FROM THE
NANCY DREW FILES

THE CASE: A crime wave has struck the River Heights warehouse district—and Nancy suspects an inside job.

CONTACT: Tom Hayward, *the handsome young CEO of Hayward Security, has been hired to protect all the burglarized warehouses.*

SUSPECTS: Stanley Loomis—*part owner of a competing company, he'd like nothing better than to see the upstart Hayward take a fall.*

Adam Reeves—*a security guard employed by Hayward, he has had ample opportunity to case each of the warehouses.*

Neil Masterson—*a vice president of Hayward Security, he is in desperate need of quick cash for his family.*

COMPLICATIONS: Not only does Nancy have to catch a thief, she also has to keep reporter Brenda Carlton from getting in the way and watch out for the safety of the girl who keeps tagging along, wanting to assist her.

Books in The Nancy Drew Files™ Series

Available from ARCHWAY Paperbacks

THE NANCY DREW FILES™

Case 52
DANGER FOR HIRE

CAROLYN KEENE

AN ARCHWAY PAPERBACK
Published by POCKET BOOKS
New York   London   Toronto   Sydney   Tokyo   Singapore

AN ARCHWAY PAPERBACK *Original*

An Archway Paperback published by
POCKET BOOKS, a division of Simon & Schuster Inc.
1230 Avenue of the Americas, New York, NY 10020

ISBN: 0-671-70029-4

First Archway Paperback printing October 1990

10 9 8 7 6 5 4 3 2 1

DANGER
FOR HIRE

Chapter

One

So IN CONCLUSION, I repeat that detective work is exciting," reported Nancy Drew, "but it can also be very dangerous. Okay, does anyone have any questions?"

A dozen hands shot into the air. It was Saturday and Career Day for juniors and seniors at River Heights High School, and Nancy was one of three guest speakers discussing careers in law enforcement.

Nancy pointed to a pretty girl sitting in the front row. "Miss Drew," the girl began.

"Please! Call me Nancy," she said, brushing her reddish blond hair away from her face. At eighteen she didn't feel old enough to be a "Miss Drew." "Please tell me your name, too," she added.

The girl smiled. "It's Cindy Larson. Nancy, how do you get your cases? Do you advertise?"

"No," Nancy answered. "Usually people come to me with a problem, and more often than not there's a mystery involved."

"Well, you do have a reputation for solving tough puzzles. Like the Nikki Masters investigation. You know, there's still something about that case that I don't understand. . . . "

She launched into a long and technical question about the evidence. Nancy listened carefully and then began a quick summary of the clues.

Cindy's interest in that particular case wasn't surprising. Nikki Masters was a popular junior at River Heights High, who had been suspected of killing her boyfriend. Nancy thought of that case as *The Suspect Next Door*.

No, Cindy's interest wasn't unusual. What surprised Nancy was that the girl had such detailed recall of the case. It had happened ages ago! She must have studied the newspaper accounts very carefully. Nancy asked if there were other questions.

Nancy answered them all patiently, until she noticed that the session was almost over.

"Doesn't anyone have a question for Chief McGinnis or Tom Hayward?" Nancy asked, glancing at her two fellow speakers.

Chief McGinnis studied her with a grin. "I doubt it, Nancy. Your sleuthing sounds much more glamorous than police work. Why, I'm wondering if I should go private myself."

"The River Heights Police Department couldn't get along without you, Chief," Nancy said, her cheeks hot. "Besides, police work must be very rewarding."

"Does that mean you'll take the patrolman's exam when you're old enough?" the chief asked.

"Not so fast, Chief," Tom Hayward cut in with a devilish smile. "If anyone's going to recruit Nancy Drew, I want it to be Hayward Security Systems. My company is growing fast, and I need a bright mind like Nancy's. What do you say, Nancy? You'll earn a lot more money working for me than for the River Heights Police!"

Nancy studied Tom. He was remarkably

young to be the president of one of the most successful businesses in River Heights. Nancy knew that he was only in his midtwenties and easily the youngest millionaire in River Heights.

He's probably the most handsome, too, Nancy decided. Tall and athletic, with neatly trimmed sandy blond hair and attractive steel blue eyes, Tom was the all-American dreamboat. Furthermore, his smile was warm and his manner was easy. No wonder he was so successful! Nancy liked him the moment she met him. It was hard not to.

"I don't know," she said and smiled in response to his job offer. "Security is a whole different ball game than solving mysteries."

Tom smiled back and turned to face the students. "I hope that when you finally make a career choice, you will consider the security business. It pays well and there's plenty of opportunity for advancement."

Nancy listened in admiration as he shifted smoothly into a final pitch for his firm.

"In fact," he went on, "I am hiring right now for Hayward Security Guard Services. So far not one of our customers' homes or businesses has been robbed. So think about Hayward, okay? Especially you graduating seniors."

Just then a bell rang, signaling the end of the session. As the students rose and began filing out, Nancy turned to Tom and the chief. "Well, how'd we do?"

"I'd say you did well, Nancy," the chief answered. "I'll bet every one of those kids wants to be a PI."

It was probably true. A few students were hanging back, and they were all gathered around Nancy. Blushing, Nancy fielded their queries one at a time. The last of the group was Cindy Larson.

Cindy was of average height, slim, with an athletic build. Her face was pretty in an innocent, hometown-sweetheart way. Her gray eyes were bright and intelligent, and her glossy brown hair was shoulder-length and stylishly cut. She was dressed to impress, like most of the students, but Nancy got the feeling that she'd be more at home in jeans.

"That was a good question you had about the Nikki Masters case," Nancy complimented her. "Did you follow it in the papers?"

"Oh, I save *all* the articles about your cases," Cindy said. "I keep them in a binder, a sort of casebook. See?"

She handed Nancy a notebook. Opening it, Nancy was amazed to see that it contained a complete set of newspaper clippings about her. Some of the articles went back several years! Stunned, Nancy realized that this girl was a fan of hers—big time.

Nancy felt both flattered and oddly uneasy. Fans were for movie stars, not teenage detectives. She closed the album and handed it back to the girl.

"I'm honored," she said gratefully.

"No, *I'm* honored," Cindy answered. "I think you are totally amazing. I mean, a hundred other people could have the same clues that you have on a case, but you're the one who puts them all together and catches the crook."

"Oh, I usually have lots of help," Nancy demurred.

"Not always. You must be incredibly smart."

"No, just persistent," Nancy said with an uneasy smile. She was definitely feeling uncomfortable now. It was obvious that the girl idolized her—or at least had an exaggerated mental picture of her. That was too bad. She was bound to be disappointed by the real-life Nancy Drew. Nancy felt that she was a pretty ordinary person most of the time.

"Okay, so you're persistent *and* smart!" her

fan agreed. "That still means you're incredible. My goal is to be a detective, too. Your life sounds so exciting."

"Lots of times it is," Nancy admitted. "But some of the time it's downright scary."

"You always come out of your cases okay, though."

"So far! I've been lucky," Nancy said sincerely.

"It's more than luck. You know how to keep your cool," Cindy insisted.

"I'm also well trained in a lot of stuff, like judo and fencing and—" Nancy stopped herself. She was beginning to sound as if she were bragging!

"I want to learn all that stuff, too," Cindy announced.

Nancy nodded. "Then do it. You'll enjoy it. I know I did. But if you're going to be a detective, you have to learn that there are times when the work is dull—with a capital *D*."

"Oh, I'm sure it could never be dull!" Cindy said with a grin.

It was hopeless. Cindy was determined to glamorize Nancy, so Nancy decided to quit trying to set the girl straight.

Just then they were startled by the loud crackle of the chief's radio. "Headquarters to PO One. Are you there, Chief?"

At that same moment, Tom Hayward's beeper began to chirp. Shutting it off, Tom swiveled to face the others. "Excuse me."

He left the room to find a phone. The chief, meanwhile, lifted his black police radio from its leather holster at his waist. He punched the transmit button. "Chief here."

"Chief." The radio crackled again. "We need you down at Orange and Duke. We got a major five-five-oh at that location."

"Anyone injured?" the chief demanded.

"Negative. An S.G. was gift wrapped, that's all."

"I'm all done here. Be right down," the chief said. "Over and out."

Nancy grinned at the chief. "A big warehouse burglary, huh? Must have been a professional job—that is, since a security guard was bound and gagged."

The chief shook his head in admiration. "No one slips anything over on you, Nancy."

"Sometimes, but not *usually*. Anyway, thank goodness no one was hurt," Nancy commented.

"No one but me!" said a male voice from the doorway.

Nancy, Cindy, and the chief wheeled around to face Tom Hayward, who had come back into the room.

"That was a call from my office," he said in a hollow voice. "The warehouse that was robbed is guarded by Hayward. So much for our perfect record! I'm ruined!"

Chapter

Two

"THAT'S TERRIBLE," Nancy said, her blue eyes expressing concern. "About the burglary, I mean. It's not really the end of Hayward Security, though, is it?"

"I'm afraid it might be," Tom lamented. "You see, the whole foundation of our business is our complete reliability. The state-of-the-art alarm systems we put in, plus our security guard service, let our customers feel safe. If they don't feel safe anymore, then *poof!*—we have nothing left."

"One break-in isn't going to shatter the confidence of your customers," Nancy suggested.

"It won't help it."

"But no one's perfect." Nancy searched for a way to help him feel better. "In fact, a break-in was probably inevitable sometime," she said. "And this obviously was the work of professionals."

"That's even worse," Tom moaned. He began to pack his briefcase. "It's the pros that our systems are supposed to thwart. This is a disaster."

Nancy gave herself a mental kick—she had only succeeded in making him feel worse.

"Let's not call this a disaster yet," the chief said. "Maybe these 'pros' weren't so professional after all. If we catch them—"

"Sure!" Nancy interrupted. "If they're put in jail, your company's reputation will hardly suffer at all."

"I guess," Tom said, not convinced at all.

"Well, let's get going," the chief said. "We won't know anything until we check out the scene. Care to come, Nancy?"

"You bet." Nancy turned to her student admirer. "It was nice talking to you. I hope you make your dream come true and become a detective. I could use some company!"

A second later she was halfway to the door.

Nancy shifted her Mustang and let it glide downhill. It wasn't hard to figure out where to go. A herd of blue-and-white police cars jammed the street in front of a warehouse, their twin roof lights twirling. The long, low warehouse had *CD Revolution* painted in giant red letters across its front.

On her way inside, Nancy noticed the high-tech alarm and lock system that controlled the loading bay door. There was even a control panel on the wall outside. Unusual. With access to the system so easy, Tom was obviously confident that the system was secure. So what had gone wrong?

Tom and the chief were in the glass-enclosed inner office, questioning the security guard who had been tied up by the robbers. A plainclothes detective was taking notes. Nancy, not wanting to intrude, waited outside the door.

"No, I never saw their faces," the young guard was saying. "They were wearing masks."

"Ski masks?" the detective asked.

"No, rubber Halloween masks. You know, the kind that pull over your whole head. Frankenstein, the Mummy . . . like that."

"Gloves?" the chief asked.

"Yeah, cloth. Work gloves."

"Weapons?" Tom inquired.

"Uh—long-barrel automatics."

Professionals, Nancy thought. Eager to ask her own questions, she was glad when the chief noticed her.

"Ah, Nancy! Come in," he said. "You're good at spotting things. Take a look around and see what you find."

Nodding to Tom and the detective, Nancy slid inside and quickly asked, "How much was taken?"

"We're not sure yet," Tom said. "It looks like about two hundred boxes of CDs were lifted. They backed a truck to the loading dock and moved the boxes with handcarts. The whole operation took only seven minutes."

"I timed them on the wall clock," the guard chimed in.

"Fast work," Nancy commented.

"They didn't bother to blindfold me. They didn't have to," said the guard, sounding morose.

14

"Because of the masks." Nancy nodded. "How did they get inside in the first place?" she asked curiously.

"They came in through the loading bay door. All of a sudden I saw it rolling up, but by the time I got there, two of 'em had rolled underneath and had their guns pointed at me. They tied me up, and—bingo. Seven minutes later they were out of here. That was it."

Nancy narrowed her eyes. "Wait a minute. . . . How did they disable the alarm connected to the loading bay door? To turn it off you'd need a code, and I'll bet you get only one chance to input the correct code on the keypad."

"That's right," Tom supplied.

They all looked at the guard. He shifted uncomfortably. He was tall and athletic and quite young. Nineteen at the most, Nancy guessed. The name tag sewn on his gray uniform said "Adam Reeves."

The police detective shot them all a warning look. He was obviously suspicious of the guard, but wanted to take it slow with him. "Okay, let's get back to the robbers," he said. "Did they say anything to you?"

After a minute a pair of uniformed officers

entered. With them was a worried-looking woman holding a thick computer printout and a pencil.

"We've done a preliminary check of the inventory," she said. She must be the warehouse manager, Nancy realized, called in on her day off. "There are about two hundred and twenty-five cartons of CDs missing. They seem to have picked whatever was closest to the door," she added.

"That's strange," Nancy commented. "You'd think they'd take only best-sellers." Especially considering how well they planned the rest of the operation, she added to herself.

A commotion outside the office interrupted them. A patrolman was attempting to block the path of a dark-haired young woman. She was about eighteen, Nancy's age, and was angrily waving an ID card in their faces.

"I'm with the press," she snapped. "I demand that you let me through!"

Oh, no! Nancy thought. Brenda Carlton!

Nancy could see that the teenage reporter looked as professional as ever in a tailored skirt and pumps. If only Brenda would pay less attention to her appearance and more to responsible reporting, Nancy thought wearily. Their paths had crossed often, and once too often Brenda had come close to ruining Nancy's investigations. She had even put their lives in danger.

Dropping one shoulder like a linebacker, Brenda rudely shoved past the officer. She was firing off a rapid string of questions as she burst into the office.

Adam Reeves glanced at Tom, who shook his head. He didn't want his guard answering any questions.

"Um . . . I don't think I should comment," Adam said.

"Chief, what about you? What steps are you taking?"

Nancy pressed her lips together to keep from smiling. Brenda was such a cartoon! Of course, she thought of herself as an ace reporter. The truth was that she had a byline only because her father was the owner and publisher of *Today's Times.*

The chief rolled his eyes. He was well acquainted with Brenda's blunt style. "Our investigation is continuing," he told her. "Other than that, I have no comment."

Brenda turned to Tom. "What about you, Mr. Hayward? This break-in is a big setback for your firm. . . ."

Nancy caught the chief's eye and inclined

her head in the direction of the door. The chief took the hint, and both of them slipped quietly into the warehouse proper.

"Chief," Nancy said in a low voice, "if you ask me, these crooks had inside help. Someone gave them the code to that alarm."

"Looks like it," the chief agreed. "We'll work on that angle."

A moment later Tom joined them, having left Brenda to Adam and the detective. "Chief, I've got a big problem," he said with a cautious backward glance.

"I know," the chief said. "Nancy and I were just discussing that. It will take some in-depth probing to uncover the person in your operation who helped these robbers, which is a bit beyond us right now. We've had a big budget cut."

"Yeah, I know," Tom said. He didn't sound bitter, however. "Looks like I'll have to do that work myself."

The chief rubbed the side of his nose with his index finger. "May I make a suggestion?"

"Please," Tom said.

"Since it'll be difficult for you to be objective about your own people, why not get some outside help? I know someone who's already familiar with the case. . . . "

"You mean *Nancy?*" Tom sounded startled.

"Naturally." The chief smiled at her. "She's got a nose for the truth, and a brain that thrives on mysteries. She'll be perfect—if she wants to take the case."

"Oh, I do," Nancy said quickly. She didn't have to think twice.

Tom studied her for a moment, probably wondering if an eighteen-year-old could really help him. A lot of people wondered that at first.

Finally he nodded. After all, he was not that much older than she. "Thanks, Nancy. Why not meet me at my office? I'll pull out some employee records, and we can make plans."

Nancy smiled. She always felt great when she got a new case. "Okay. I think I'll take a last look around here first, though."

"Sure. I've got a few details to wrap up, too," Tom said.

Nancy walked into the heart of the warehouse. There were aisles and aisles of industrial metal shelves. Each shelf, in turn, was packed with cardboard boxes. Glued to each box was a computer-generated label that announced its contents in large letters. It was easy to see which CDs were where. Why had the robbers chosen their loot at random?

19

Puzzled, Nancy moved still deeper into the building. The only noise she could hear was the soft buzzing of the strip lighting overhead. It was very quiet.

Scrape.

Off to her left, Nancy heard a shoe scuff against the concrete floor. A police officer? No, they were all in the front of the warehouse, waiting for orders.

The next sound was faint—but unmistakable. Someone was walking slowly and quietly. Nancy was not alone.

Chapter

Three

NANCY PEERED THROUGH the gap between two shelves, her heart beating faster. Two aisles away she caught a flash of movement. A jade-colored shirt? After slipping off her shoes, she crept ahead.

At the corner she paused and was just in time to see a lithe figure dart around the corner at the far end of the aisle.

Crouching low, Nancy took a chance and ran forward as quickly as she could. When she was halfway to the front of the warehouse, she turned left and zipped up an aisle. Good, thought Nancy. The figure was coming toward her.

Nancy waited until the figure was only a few feet away. Then she turned the corner and stood directly in the figure's path.

"Cindy Larson, what are *you* doing here?"

"Aaagh!" With a howl of fright, Cindy scrambled backward. She struggled for balance as she stumbled into a stack of boxes. "Nancy, you scared me to death!"

Nancy suppressed a smile. "Sorry. I wasn't sure it was you at first. Now, you'd better tell me what you're doing. Do the police know you're in here?"

"Well, sort of," Cindy said in embarrassment. "See, I really wanted to come get a look at an actual crime scene, so I came here and told the police officers that I had a message for you. They told me you were back here, and I . . . well, I felt dumb because I *didn't* have a message for you, but I wanted to watch you work anyway, so I followed you back here hoping that you wouldn't see me. I guess I didn't do a very good job of hiding, huh?"

"Of hiding, no," Nancy said. "Of getting past the police—not bad. But you shouldn't have made up a story. Especially when you could have just asked me to show you around."

"I didn't think you would."

"Oh." Nancy felt bad for coming down so hard on Cindy. An idea came to her just then. It was perfect! "Cindy, I'm going to be helping Tom Hayward get to the bottom of this robbery. Would you like to work with me on this case?"

Cindy swallowed. "Do you mean it?"

Nancy beamed. "Sure! This is the sort of case that has a lot of legwork to it . . . you know, cross-checking schedules, getting information on the phone, that kind of thing. It'd be a lot for me to handle on my own, but with a helper—"

"Oh, this is the most exciting thing that's *ever* happened to me! Wait until I tell my friends! Of course, I'll only be able to help you after school, but don't worry, Nancy! I'll be the best assistant detective you've ever had!"

That's a tall promise, Nancy thought to herself. She was usually assisted in her cases by her two best friends, Bess Marvin and George Fayne. Her boyfriend, Ned Nickerson, had been in on quite a few as well. All had proved themselves to be invaluable.

"Great," Nancy said. "Well, I'm all done here. Let's go." After retrieving her shoes, she walked outside onto the loading dock with Cindy.

"Here's my home number," Nancy said, jotting it down on a scrap of paper from her purse. "Now tell me yours, and we'll arrange—"

Screeeeeeeeeeeeeeeeeeeeeeeeeech!

The air was split by an ear-shattering burst of feedback. Nancy's hands flew to her ears.

As suddenly as the noise had begun, it stopped. Then from the loudspeakers above the loading platform across the street came a booming, gleeful voice. "So! How does it feel, Tom Hayward, you little creep! Not a lot of fun to have a client robbed, is it?"

Nancy's gaze swung across the street as Tom and the chief appeared beside her. Brenda was not far behind them.

"About time you had a setback, son. It'll make you humble. Make you think twice about taking away other people's business! I'll tell you another thing, too, Hayward—I'm glad. You're getting exactly what you deserve!"

The chief yelled, "Bates! Go find out who that is!"

"Wait," Tom said, laying a hand on the chief's outstretched arm. "I know who it is.

It's Stanley Loomis. My main rival. Stanley's had the security business in River Heights all to himself for years—until I came along."

"He's not happy about your success, obviously," the chief observed.

That was the understatement of the year, in Nancy's opinion. The amplified tirade continued for a few minutes longer, and then abruptly ceased. A moment later a metal door on the opposite loading platform opened, and a portly man wearing brown slacks and a plaid sports jacket emerged.

He said nothing. He just climbed into a large tan luxury car and roared away.

"That's Loomis," Tom said. "He overcharged his clients for years. Now I'm offering people better service at a lower price, and he resents it."

Nancy wondered if it was possible that Stanley Loomis had arranged the robbery. Yes, she decided almost instantly. Proving it, though, was going to take some work.

That evening at dinner Nancy told her father, Carson Drew, about Tom's remark. They were sitting at the dinner table with Hannah Gruen, their longtime housekeeper, eating pot roast.

"You're right—that wouldn't have done any

good," Carson said. "Hayward's just discouraged. This is his first big setback."

"He's awfully young, isn't he?" Hannah remarked. "He's not used to business difficulties, I'll bet. But he'll learn. With more experience, problems like this won't bother him so much."

Nancy's father lifted the salt shaker from the table. "I guess he needs more 'seasoning,' eh, Hannah?"

Nancy groaned. "Dad, that was your worst pun in a week."

"Just trying to add some spice to the discussion," Carson quipped.

"Ohhh!" Nancy moaned, rolling her eyes.

"Mr. Drew, you shouldn't joke about it," Hannah scolded. "Tom Hayward is in trouble. He needs help, and I think it's wonderful that Nancy is giving it to him."

Nancy smiled. "Thanks, Hannah. It remains to be seen whether I'll be much help, though."

"I'm sure you will," her father said, setting the salt shaker down again. "In fact, you have one suspect already, don't you? That young guard . . . what was his name?"

"Adam Reeves."

"He seems a likely bet."

"Sure," Nancy agreed. "I'll be checking up on him as soon as I can."

Carson wiped his mouth on his white linen napkin. "There's something I don't understand. If Adam Reeves was tied to a chair, who called the police?"

"He did—in a way," Nancy explained. "The chair the robbers tied him to had wheels. He waited until they were gone, then he rolled himself to a side exit and butted open the door. It had a bar lever. so he didn't have to use his hands."

"How did he untie himself?" Hannah asked.

"He didn't. The emergency exit had a separate alarm connected to it. The alarm went off. and a patrol car stopped to investigate. The two officers untied him and called headquarters."

"Hmm. That's how Brenda found out about it. too." Carson surmised. "Monitoring the police channel."

"Obviously," Nancy agreed.

Hannah rose and began clearing the dishes. "Who'd like cherry pie?"

"None for me," Nancy said. folding her napkin and rising. "It sounds fantastic, but I don't want to be slowed down by a full stomach tonight."

"Going dancing with Ned?" her father asked.

"No, he's staying on campus this weekend,"

Nancy answered a little wistfully. Her boyfriend was a student at Emerson College and didn't get home very often. "I'm going to begin some surveillance of the warehouse district. I have a hunch that we haven't seen the last of these robbers."

"Are you sure that's a good idea? Especially at night?" Carson asked.

"I'll be careful. If they show up again, I'll phone the police," Nancy promised.

In the daytime the warehouse district was crowded with trucks and warehouse workers. At night, though, the area was quiet and seemed sinister, the occasional streetlight dropping an isolated white cone of light into the darkness.

Nancy drove once through the entire grid of streets, carefully noting the location of pay phones and fire boxes. Then she parked near the river, not far from the fat silver grain silos and began to patrol on foot.

She was wearing black jeans, black sneakers, and a worn leather jacket that Ned had given her. It was chilly out. Nancy zipped her jacket to her chin and flipped up the collar.

Late-night deliveries were under way at a few of the warehouses, but most were dark, their loading bays closed with metal security doors. Nancy was pretty sure she'd be able to tell if a robbery was under way—a truck would be loading at one or another of the bays, but the work would be done with flashlights. She saw nothing suspicious.

After an hour she had worked her way around half the streets. The next block was a long one. Nancy walked down it quickly. All of the warehouses were dark. If she were looking for a place to rob, this was definitely a block she'd be interested in.

Then, passing an alley, she thought she heard a faint sound.

Nancy paused. Alert for the slightest noise, she peered down the alley. There was nothing but some garbage dumpsters, a few stacks of crates, and a door set into one wall. Nancy waited.

Creak.

There! No mistaking it that time. Something —or someone—had made a sound. She started down the alley, then stopped.

Silence. Nancy tiptoed farther. She kept near to the wall because it was darker there. She paused again, letting her eyes adjust to the alley's blackness.

Still no sound. Nancy crept one step farther and stopped behind a ten-foot-high stack of wooden crates.

Creeeeeeeak!

She was close now. But where was the noise coming from?

Suddenly Nancy froze—and raised her eyes. The stack of crates was falling toward her. In less than a second she'd be crushed!

Chapter

Four

WITH A SCREAM, Nancy dived to her right. She tucked and rolled as the crates hit the pavement where she had been standing a second earlier.

The top ones splintered and sent a blizzard of white Styrofoam peanuts into the alley. As Nancy began to rise, a dark figure raced past her, shoving her violently to the ground.

"Hey! Stop!" Nancy shouted, but it was futile. She looked up just in time to see a dark shape zoom out of the alley and wheel left.

She was furious. There had been no need to

try to hurt her. Whoever it was had only needed to stand still in the shadows. In a minute or two she would have gone away.

Nancy took off at a sprint and turned left at the top of the alley. The figure was fifty yards ahead of her. As the figure crossed through a pool of light below a street lamp, Nancy saw that he—it was definitely a he—was wearing black. A rubber mask of some sort was pulled over his head.

She ran flat out. Unfortunately, her attacker was even faster than she was. Nancy couldn't keep up. Her heart was hammering and her shoulder was throbbing. She tried to put on speed, but it wasn't enough.

As she turned the second corner she groaned. The street was empty except for a car a couple of blocks away that was careening around a corner. Nancy watched in anger as her attacker's red brake lights flared for a second, then winked out.

He was gone. Nancy stood panting, her breath sending little clouds of vapor into the frigid air. She felt frustrated and unsettled. Maybe her attacker had been checking out a robbery target, but a nagging suspicion told her that his purpose was different. He had been waiting for her, and she had walked right into his trap.

The next morning was bright and sunny—a perfect fall day. As Nancy descended the stairs, though, she still felt uneasy about the night before. Had she been set up? She still wasn't sure.

Hannah had a pancake breakfast waiting. Her father was already at the table.

"How'd the surveillance go?" Carson asked, smiling over the top of his newspaper.

Nancy shrugged. "I'm not sure. I think I ran into one of the robbers."

Carson put down his newspaper. "Are you okay?"

"I'm fine," Nancy promised.

"I thought you weren't going to tangle with them. You said you were going to call—"

"The police. Yes, I know," Nancy said, feeling a bit guilty. "I didn't have time. It was over in a minute." She took her seat.

Carson frowned. "Nancy, I don't like you putting yourself in danger."

"It wasn't a dangerous situation, Dad," she said. "At least, not very," she added under her breath. The guy had merely shoved her to the ground, but he might have done worse. *Long-barrel automatics.* This gang used guns.

"Please be careful, won't you?" Carson said.

"I will," Nancy assured him with a smile. "And don't tell Hannah! She worries about me even more than you do."

"Don't tell Hannah *what?*" the housekeeper demanded, sweeping into the dining room with a pitcher of orange juice.

Nancy casually forked two pancakes onto her plate. "Nothing. It's just something . . . uh, something in the newspaper."

"You never lie well first thing in the morning," Hannah observed, taking her seat. "Your father said something about worrying. What have you been doing that would worry me?"

Nancy grinned weakly. "Uh . . . can I tell you about it this afternoon?"

Hannah sighed wearily and, to Nancy's relief, let it go at that.

After a minute Carson extended the front section of the newspaper to Nancy. He said, "Here's a story that will interest you."

Nancy glanced at the paper. "Ugh. That's Brenda's paper."

"Yes, but take a look anyway."

Nancy took the paper from him and scanned

it. The headline read, "Robbery Embarrasses Security Wizard." The byline was Brenda's.

"It figures," Nancy muttered.

She began to read. Brenda's writing style was breathless and sensational. It always irritated Nancy, and now she liked it even less. According to Brenda, the robbery was the most daring ever pulled in River Heights. The police, she stated, were baffled. No clues had been found.

"This is totally exaggerated!" Nancy complained.

"It gets worse," her father told her.

The concluding paragraph read:

Yesterday's events may be the beginning of even deeper trouble for Hayward Security Systems. A survey of the crime scene by this reporter indicates that a company insider may have aided the robbers. A well-known private investigator was also at the site, suggesting that the company is planning an inquiry by impartial outsiders.

"Oh, great," Nancy said, tossing down the paper in disgust. "Not only does she trash

Tom's company, she also tips off his employees about my investigation."

"Were you planning to work undercover?" Carson asked.

"No, but it's always nice to have the element of surprise when you interview someone," Nancy explained. "People are usually more candid when they're caught off guard."

Nancy finished her breakfast in gloomy silence. She spent most of the day in her room reviewing the employee records that Tom had given her the day before. It was boring stuff, mostly, but Nancy found two items of interest.

The first was in Adam Reeves's employment application. As Nancy had guessed, he was nineteen. He had graduated from Mapleton High School two years earlier and had worked at a gas station from February until November of the previous year. Tom's company had hired him the previous December, and except for a two-week training period, he had been in the security guard division ever since.

What, Nancy wondered, had Adam done between his graduation and the following January, when he began working at the gas station? Six months of his life was unaccounted for!

The other interesting item that Nancy found was that both the security guard division and the crews who installed the alarm systems reported to the same man—the vice-president of operations, Neil Masterson. If anyone could tell her who could obtain the alarm code, it would be he.

Nancy was resting in her room before dinner when Bess Marvin and George Fayne swept in.

"Hannah says you've got a new case," George said, breezing over to Nancy's bed and flopping down. She was trim and highly athletic. Her curly dark hair was cut functionally short, and her dark eyes sparkled.

"Why didn't you tell us?" Bess complained, crossing to Nancy's full-length mirror for a quick check of her makeup. Although they were cousins, Bess was George's opposite. Her eyes were blue, her figure was curvy, and she wore her blond hair long.

"Give me a break!" Nancy said, laughing. "I only got this case yesterday."

"Well, where do we come in?" Bess demanded.

Nancy filled them in on the details. "As for you guys—well, I may not be needing your help this time around."

"You mean we're fired?" George asked with a grin.

Bess gave her hair an exaggerated toss. "Well, talk about *gratitude!*"

"Cut it out, you guys." Nancy giggled. "After all, you're always griping that I drag you into these things against your wills. Especially you, Bess. And this time I've got the help of a volunteer."

Nancy told them about her fan, Cindy Larson, and how she promised her she could help. "This case looks so straightforward, it'll probably be boring. I'll interview the suspects, check their backgrounds, and make my report. That's it."

Bess shook her head. "Oh, sure. I've heard *that* one before."

Just then Nancy's phone rang. She lifted the handset. "Hello?"

"Nancy, it's Tom. Can you meet me? Another warehouse has been robbed!"

Chapter

Five

LEAVING BESS AND GEORGE with a hasty apology, Nancy raced to her car. The sky was twilight pink as she parked at the location Tom had given her. The warehouse in question was larger than the one that had been robbed the previous day. A sign over the loading bay door announced that it belonged to Jumping Jeans, a clothing chain.

Tom was inside with Chief McGinnis. "What happened?" Nancy asked, rushing to the inner office.

"Exactly the same thing that happened yesterday," Tom reported grimly. "The thieves got inside by disarming the alarm. It's the same gang, no question."

"Chief?" Nancy asked.

"Looks likely. Their method of operation is nearly identical. What surprises me is that they struck again so soon after their last job."

It was a bold strike. Nancy had to agree. They hadn't even waited for the "heat" to die down from the previous day.

"Where's the guard?" Nancy asked. "Did he see anything?"

Tom rubbed his temples. "Unfortunately, this warehouse isn't guarded on Sundays. The client felt that our alarm system would be enough."

"Tell me—how much did they take?" Nancy asked.

"That's the funny part," the chief said. "The warehouse manager has checked the inventory. They took only enough jeans to fill up about a quarter of your average truck."

"That's odd. They had all the time in the world," Nancy mused.

"Maybe, maybe not. They were operating in broad daylight," Tom observed.

"True, but on Sunday this area has got to be

deserted," Nancy reasoned. "If there was no guard around, who called in the complaint?"

"The robbers left the loading bay door slightly ajar when they took off. A patrol car eventually noticed and checked it out," the chief said.

"You had a car patrolling the area?" Nancy asked, surprised. If that was true, then the robbers' crime had been doubly brazen.

"Yes, and I wish I had assigned more than one," the chief said ruefully. "Unfortunately, like Tom, I didn't expect that they'd strike again so soon."

"Who did?" Nancy said sympathetically. "It looks like they'll consider making a hit anytime the area is fairly empty."

"Thank goodness it will be busy again tomorrow morning," Tom said. "I feel awful about this. And to think that I spent the day trying to relax! I was sailing on the river with some friends. I should have been at work instead."

"Don't blame yourself," Nancy advised him. "By the way, Tom, there's something I wanted to ask you. Do you remember I told you that I was going to do some surveillance last night?"

"Yes."

"Did you happen to mention my plan to anyone else?" she asked casually.

Tom frowned. "No, I don't think that I— wait a minute. I believe I mentioned it to my VP in charge of operations, Neil Masterson."

Nancy's eyebrows rose. "No one else?"

"No. Neil was the only person I talked to. How'd it go last night, anyway?" Tom asked.

"I ran into one of the gang."

"What?" the chief and Tom cried in unison.

"Where?" Tom went on.

The chief demanded, "When? And what did he look like?"

"He was tall, trim, and in excellent shape," Nancy told them. "He outran me by a mile. Other than that, I can't tell you much. He was dressed in black and had a rubber mask over his head."

"Nancy, maybe you'd better forget about doing any more surveillance," the chief said.

"But if there's a company insider involved, then he or she will keep the gang one step ahead of us all the time. My best chance of getting a line on the gang is to catch them in the act."

"I don't know, Nancy. It sounds risky," Tom said.

"Sure, but without risk there's no reward," Nancy countered.

The chief puffed out his cheeks and expelled a long breath. "Nancy, I think Tom is right. This gang seems to be fearless. From now on I want you to let me know every time you patrol the area. I'll make sure there's a cruiser around."

"Okay." Nancy nodded. She'd be glad to know that the police were standing by. She added, "With a little luck we'll put a stop to these robberies soon."

"How soon?" asked a girl's voice behind them.

Nancy turned in surprise to see Brenda furiously jotting something down on her pad. She was wearing designer jeans and an expensive brown leather jacket.

How much had Brenda heard of their conversation? Nancy wondered.

"The RHPD is continuing its investigation," the chief stated blandly. "Other than that, I have no comment."

"Mr. Hayward? Two of your customers have been robbed in one weekend. How can your other customers be certain that they won't be robbed, too?"

"Because Hayward systems are the best,

that's why," Tom said, losing some of his composure. "It's the people who rely on the other security services in town who should be concerned."

Brenda zeroed in. "Are you telling me that it's just coincidence that both robberies happened to clients of Hayward Security?"

Tom went on to defend his record. Nancy thought he was foolish to let himself be baited by Brenda. Her only interest was in getting a good story. If necessary she would twist his remarks to make him say anything she wanted.

Leaving them, Nancy privately told the chief of her destination and headed off to search the alley where she had been attacked the night before.

At nine the next morning, Nancy swung her Mustang into an empty parking space at Hayward Security Systems. Her examination of the alley the night before had revealed nothing, and she was now determined to try a fresh angle. The company's headquarters were in a low steel and tinted glass building in an office park on the outskirts of River Heights. She locked her car and walked to the front doors, which whooshed open automatically.

Inside, she was escorted to the office of Neil Masterson. He was in his early thirties, tall and dark haired. He seemed remarkably relaxed, given what had happened over the weekend. His handshake was firm and friendly.

Before Nancy took a seat opposite his desk, she noticed a framed photo on his desk.

"That's my wife and daughter," Neil said proudly, turning the photo so Nancy could see the pretty woman and laughing baby girl. "Tasha—that's my daughter—is eighteen months old."

"She's cute."

"Smart, too. Do I sound biased?" he asked with a grin.

"No, of course not." Nancy smiled, too, in spite of herself.

Leaning back in his desk chair, Neil got down to business. "Tom said that you're doing an independent investigation. That's great. An outside opinion is definitely called for under the circumstances. How can I help?"

"I need some information about the alarm system at the two warehouses. For instance, who makes up the access codes?"

"It's not 'who' but 'what.'" Neil answered. Swiveling, he patted the computer that occu-

pied one corner of his desk. "This is pro-
grammed with a random code generator. Once
a month it changes the access codes for each of
our customers' alarm systems by telephone."

"Then how do the guards and the warehouse
managers find out the code?" Nancy inquired.

"Do you see that printer over there?"

Nancy spotted a computer printer to her
left. A string of envelopes was rolled into it.
The envelopes were the type with carbon paper
lining and tissue-thin sheets of paper sealed
inside, so that a message could be printed
without having to open the envelope.

"When the computer assigns a new code,"
Neil continued, "it prints a sealed copy. Once
a month the guards and the warehouse manager report to this office in person, and I hand
them the envelope. They memorize the code.
Then I run the envelope through our shred-
der."

"I see," Nancy said. "What happens if a
guard calls in sick? Or the warehouse gets a
new manager? Do you print out extra copies of
the code for their replacements?"

"Well—no. I have to print a new envelope,
of course, but when I do, the computer gener-
ates a new code."

Nancy nodded. "Clever. Whoever designed

this system seems to have thought of everything. It sounds amazingly secure."

"We thought so, too—until this weekend."

Nancy frowned. "So if only authorized users have access to the codes, then only an insider could be behind these thefts," she said after a moment.

"Unfortunately, that's the only possible explanation," Neil confirmed.

"Well, the next step, I guess, is to see if there is anyone who worked at both warehouses," Nancy said.

Neil tapped a yellow legal pad on his desk. "I started working on that angle this morning," he said.

"And?"

"Well," Neil said, "there's only one name that crops up at both locations. It's one of our guards, I'm afraid."

"Adam Reeves, right?" Nancy guessed excitedly.

"Yes."

She grinned. "Then he's our man!"

"Not necessarily," Neil said cautiously. "You see, he was assigned to the Jumping Jeans warehouse for only one month. The alarm code has changed several times since then."

"But perhaps he or another member of the gang bribed someone to leak it. What's your opinion of Adam Reeves?"

Neil shrugged. "We screen our employees very carefully. Other than that, I really can't say. I hardly know the guy. I assume he's okay, though. He's been working here longer than I have."

"I see," she said thoughtfully.

After chatting for a few more minutes, Nancy thanked him and left. To get to the bottom of this, she realized, she would have to dig much deeper.

Nancy's home was in one of the nicest neighborhoods in River Heights. It was an area of broad streets lined with graceful trees, sweeping lawns, and large houses.

As Nancy pulled into her driveway, she saw that her father's car was parked there. What was he doing at home on a Monday? she wondered. After shutting off the engine, she leaped out of her car and walked around the house to the kitchen door.

Hannah was in the kitchen. "Your father's working in his study," she reported. "Some corporate work, I gather."

"Poor Dad," Nancy said sympathetically.

Nancy's father was a well-known lawyer whose first love was criminal cases. Still, he did some corporate work, as the hefty fees paid by his corporate clients were hard to turn down. He did take the work, but grumbled whenever he did.

Nancy tapped on the door of his study and went in. Her father was talking on the phone. He waved her into one of the leather chairs opposite his desk.

"Incredible," he was saying into the phone. "Down two points in one hour? That'll mean some problems for—"

The person at the other end of the line began to speak. Carson nodded, then frowned, then shook his head sadly.

"Well, keep me posted," he said finally. "Goodbye."

"What's going on?" Nancy asked as her father hung up.

"That was my stockbroker in Chicago," he said. "He called with some information I requested, but then we began to chat. He told me that Brenda Carlton's latest article about Tom Hayward has been picked up by a wire service, and it ran in this morning's Chicago papers."

Carson went on. "The article makes it sound

49

like Tom's company is in bad trouble. Investors are dumping their shares in Hayward Security right and left."

"Bad news, huh?" Nancy asked, concerned.

Carson nodded. "You bet. The price of a share has dropped almost twenty-five percent this morning alone. Since Tom is the majority shareholder, that means he has lost a small fortune."

Nancy gulped. "How much?"

"I'd say"—Carson took a breath—"a quarter of a million dollars at least!"

Chapter

Six

YOU'RE KIDDING!" Nancy exclaimed. "He lost a quarter of a million dollars in a few *hours?"*

"Yes."

Nancy was incredulous. "Dad, how can that be? Tom's *company* isn't losing money—not yet, anyway. And it didn't shrink in size overnight, either."

Her father nodded. "True, but that company is owned by its shareholders. Those shareholders value their stock only as long as Tom's company is able to show a profit."

"So what you're saying is that when the outlook for future profits goes down, the stock loses its value."

"Right. And because Tom's fortune is tied up in his own stock, he's losing like crazy."

Nancy whistled. "Boy, that means in another day or two Tom could be broke!"

After lunch Nancy started to dig. Her first calls were to the two warehouse managers. Both gave her descriptions and lot numbers of the goods that had been stolen. Stolen merchandise was usually sold, and that meant that it could be traced. It was a starting point, anyway.

Next, she rechecked the backgrounds of the guards currently assigned to the warehouses in question. She already knew about Adam Reeves, but he was only one of three guards regularly assigned to the CD Revolution warehouse. Jumping Jeans also had three regular guards. Except for the six months "missing" out of Adam's life, they each had spotless records and excellent references.

She was copying names and numbers from the phone book when Cindy Larson arrived after school.

"*This* is your room?" Cindy asked as Hannah showed her in. "Gosh, it's so—"

"Ordinary?" Nancy supplied.

"Yeah. I sort of expected—I don't know, a crime lab or something."

"I'd love to have one, but then where would I keep my stereo?" Nancy joked.

"Okay, how do I start?" Cindy asked.

"First, we'll try to find the stolen goods and trace them backward," Nancy said.

"You mean we're going *shopping?*" Cindy asked in amazement. "All right! And you said that detective work was dull."

Nancy grinned. "Don't get out your wallet yet. We'll be doing our 'shopping' by phone. I've made a list of local odd-lot retailers," Nancy said. "That means they carry merchandise that didn't sell at full-price stores. A few of them may also sell 'hot' goods. You're going to call them up looking for specific jeans and CDs."

"So if they've got what I'm looking for, we go check to see if the stuff came from the stolen lots, right?" Cindy concluded.

"You got it." Nancy was pleased.

Cindy smiled. "You mentioned two things. What's the other one?"

"We're going to research and write a profile of Adam Reeves," Nancy announced.

"Uh-oh," Cindy said. "This sounds like homework."

Nancy smiled and opened a drawer to pull out a sheet of stationery for a business called Highway Auto Supply. It had no address.

Cindy's eyes went wide. "What are we going to do with *that?*"

"Get Adam's credit history," Nancy explained. "Find out about his debts, credit cards, bank accounts—stuff like that. We want to know how much money he spends and where he spends it."

"Nancy, that's so personal! Who's going to tell us all that?" Cindy wondered.

Nancy leaned back in her chair. She was proud of this idea. "A credit bureau. We claim that Adam wants to open a charge account at our 'store,' and we want to know if he is a good credit risk. The bureau will tell us—in great detail—for a fee."

"Wow, I had no idea."

Nancy's tone grew determined. "Cindy, that's just the beginning. By the time we're done, we'll know things about Adam that *he's* forgotten."

* * *

They worked until dinnertime and then Cindy left.

Nancy drove back to the warehouse district because that was where she would have the best chance of getting a lead on the gang.

Before going she informed the chief, as she had promised. Two cruisers would be in the area all night.

Nancy had a large-scale map of the area from the city assessor's office with her. It showed each building, and Nancy had used a green marker to highlight those that were guarded by Hayward Security Systems. About a third of the buildings on the map were highlighted.

A light drizzle was falling when Nancy turned into the warehouse district. She flicked on her wipers and slowly drove through the streets. Within ten minutes she passed both patrol cars. As she did she turned her headlights off and on to identify herself.

The patrol cars answered with their lights. She felt good knowing that help was near.

Two hours later she decided she'd see more on foot. She parked near a cluster of fifty-gallon oil drums. Pulling up the collar of her leather jacket, she set out. Her sneakers squished on the wet pavement.

Finally, around 1:30 A.M., Nancy gave up and walked back to her car.

Slipping her key into the door, she unlocked it and climbed in. Her neck felt stiff. She rolled her head to stretch the muscles.

Nancy started the engine and snapped on the headlights. Something was different.

She tensed.

What was it?

A box was strapped to the fifty-gallon drum directly in front of her. Taped to the box with thick silver duct tape were two cylinders made of waxy red paper. Plastic wires looped from the cylinders to the box.

A bomb! Without a moment's thought Nancy slammed her car into reverse and jammed the accelerator pedal to the floor. Someone wanted her off this case in a major way!

Her tires shrieked. The Mustang fishtailed backward. Before she had gone ten feet, however, the world in front of her windshield erupted into a sea of white-hot flame.

Chapter

Seven

FOR A FEW BLINDING SECONDS the air outside the car boiled like the surface of the sun. Nancy felt her heart hammering in her chest. She was terrified.

But the Mustang was still racing backward. Fifty yards later she hit the brakes, yanked the ignition key out of its slot, and leaped out.

There were two patches of flame on the hood of her car. Nancy whipped off her jacket and beat the flames until they went out.

She heard the loud crackling of the burning

drum and watched as the one next to it ignited. Then a third caught. Nancy crouched. Off in the distance sirens began to wail. A patrol car screeched around a corner several blocks away and came flying toward her, its roof lights strobing. She started to tremble as the enormity of what had almost happened to her began to sink in.

The patrol doors of the patrol car flew open as it skidded to a stop on the wet pavement. "Are you okay?" an officer yelled as she ran toward the detective.

"Yes—no! Well, I'm not sure. I guess I am," Nancy said in a shaky voice.

"You look okay," the woman said, shining a flashlight in her face. The flashlight's beam swung to the Mustang. "Your car will need a new paint job, though."

Nancy smiled weakly. "It deserves it. That car saved my life."

"What happened?"

"A bomb was strapped to one of those oil drums," Nancy explained. "Whoever planted it must have been waiting nearby with a remote-control detonator, because a few seconds after I started my car, it went off."

"Then the guy might still be in the area!"

The officer quickly lifted her radio from her belt.

"Forget it," Nancy said, suddenly feeling angry at herself. "He's gone by now."

A few seconds later a fire engine arrived. The fire fighters quickly contained the blaze by spraying the area with chemicals. Nancy repeated her story for the fire chief, several detectives, and finally, Chief McGinnis. "That gang of thieves is definitely on to me," she concluded.

"Perhaps they saw you patrolling the area," the chief suggested.

Nancy shook her head. "I don't think so. If they did, why didn't I see *them?* No, I'm pretty sure they were told where to find me."

The chief's eyebrows drew together. "Who told them, do you think?"

Nancy gazed upward. The rain was letting up. Between the clouds she could see patches of clear, starry sky.

"I'm not sure," Nancy admitted, "but I'm going to find out."

The offices of Loomis & Petersen seemed to have survived unchanged for decades. The front door led into a retail store with large wall displays of locks, alarms, and intercom systems. A salesman took Nancy's name and disappeared up a flight of stairs at the back of the store.

A minute later he returned. "Stan says go right on up."

"Thanks."

Nancy climbed to the second floor, which was as out of date as the store below. The floor was bare wood, the paint on the walls was faded, and the hall was illuminated by long strips of fluorescent lighting.

Stanley Loomis occupied a corner office. Its large windows let in plenty of the morning light and offered a beautiful view of the river. He rose, presented a beefy hand to Nancy, and settled back into an old-fashioned wooden desk chair that squeaked every time he moved.

"I've read about you," Loomis said. He reached for a package of cigars on his desk, but then changed his mind. "You seem like a smart kid. Why are you working for Hayward?"

"What makes you think I'm working for Hayward?" Nancy asked.

"C'mon! Why else would you be here? Anyway, I saw you with Chief McGinnis and that Hayward punk on Saturday."

"I see." Loomis was shrewd, Nancy decided.

"You're wasting your time here. You know that, don't you?" Loomis barked.

"What makes you say that?" Nancy asked.

"Those robberies had to be an inside job," Loomis said. "That means you should be investigating Hayward's clients, or maybe Hayward's own employees. But not me."

"I have to cover all the angles," Nancy said evenly.

Loomis laughed nastily. "And what do you think you're going to get from me? A confession? The only thing I can tell you is that those computerized systems that Hayward has been selling are about as secure as a bureau drawer. If you're covering angles, start there."

Nancy was surprised. "You're saying Tom sells crummy alarm systems?"

"Not crummy, exactly," Loomis admitted. "But they're no better than mine."

Nancy was tired of playing games. She went on the offensive. "Mr. Loomis, on Saturday you baited Tom over a warehouse loudspeaker system. How did you happen to be at that particular location that day?"

"Coincidence," Loomis said, studying his nails.

Nancy didn't believe in coincidence. "Oh, really?"

"Prove that it wasn't," he challenged.

Nancy was silent. She couldn't prove it, and he knew it.

"Oh, don't look so gloomy," Loomis said, smiling. "Look, I'll tell you why I was there—I was checking out a customer's facility for a possible upgrade of his system. I'm planning some moves that will take the wind out of Tom Hayward's sails."

Nancy speculated upon hearing this. Did his "plans" include robbing Tom's customers in order to ruin Tom's business?

"You seem to resent Tom's success," Nancy stated plainly.

"Of course I do," Loomis said. He leaned forward all of a sudden and pointed a finger at her. "Hayward tried to buy me—us—out. Us! After thirty years in business!"

Nancy kept her face impassive. Now she was getting somewhere! "But you wouldn't sell?"

"*I* won't. But my part—" Suddenly Loomis cut off. "Well, that's none of your business. Drop it."

Nancy knew that she was getting warm. Loomis was clumsily trying to hide something. Before she could dig deeper, however, there was a knock at Loomis's door. The door swung open, and a thin, gray-haired man wearing a baggy suit stormed in. He had a piece of stationery clutched tightly in his fist.

"Stanley, I won't let you send this letter to young Hayward! It's insulting. If he reads this, he'll forget all about—" Suddenly the man noticed Nancy. "Oh, I'm sorry. I didn't realize you had company."

"This is my partner, Roy Petersen," Loomis explained. "Roy, this is Nancy Drew."

Petersen's face lit up. "You're the young detective, aren't you? I'm very glad to meet you, young lady." He offered Nancy his hand. "You know, it's nice—"

"Clam up, Roy," Loomis said rudely, cutting his partner off.

"Stanley!"

"Nancy is helping Hayward investigate those robberies," Loomis said.

"Oh—yes, a terrible business," Petersen said. "I hope you can get to the bottom of it, Nancy."

Nancy listened to the exchange in fascination. The partners were as different as night and day. She also suspected that they were in the middle of a major disagreement—a disagreement that had everything to do with Tom Hayward. But what was it?

"Anyway, Stanley," Petersen went on,

"about this letter. We shouldn't be so quick to brush off young Hayward. His offer—"

Again, Loomis cut off his partner in midsentence. "Roy, I told you that subject is closed!" He quickly turned to Nancy. "Miss Drew, would you please excuse us? We have some business here—that is, unless you have more questions?"

"None for now."

After leaving Loomis & Petersen, Nancy turned her Mustang out of town and into the farmland that lay beyond the city limits. She needed time to drive and think.

Questions were swimming around in her mind. Had the thieves known in advance that she would be patrolling the warehouse district? Who had told them? Why did they steal only moderate amounts of loot? And what about the codes? How had they gotten hold of them?

More than anything else, however, she was nagged by the feeling that she had missed something during her talk with Stanley Loomis. Something he had said was more important than it seemed—but what? She couldn't figure it out.

Nancy checked her rearview mirror. A hundred yards behind her a beige-colored car was keeping pace with her. Nancy slowed down, so the car could overtake and pass her, but it didn't. She shrugged and returned to her thoughts.

A few minutes later she checked her rear-view mirror again. The car was still there. It looked familiar. Hadn't a car just like it stopped behind her at a red light back in River Heights?

She sped up. The car behind her sped up, too. Without signaling, Nancy quickly braked and swung onto another road. The car behind her turned, too.

Nancy clenched her jaw and pressed down on the gas pedal. There was no doubt about it. She was being followed.

Chapter

Eight

Nancy continued to drive normally. She didn't want to lose this tail. She wanted to identify the person.

The road rose and dipped over a series of low hills. Nancy was pleased to spot a barn roof over the next hill. A farm was just what she needed.

As Nancy topped the rise, she jammed the gas pedal to the floor, and in a few seconds she reached the farm. Swiftly she braked and swung into the muddy yard on the far side of the barn. When she was out of sight, she turned so that the Mustang was again facing the road.

A few seconds later the other car raced past her position. It was going much faster than before. The driver was obviously panic-stricken because Nancy was no longer in sight.

Smiling in satisfaction, Nancy gunned her engine, swung onto the road, and zoomed off the way she had come. As she topped the rise, she glanced in her rearview mirror. The other car was about a hundred yards beyond the farm, doing a hasty three-point turn in the middle of the road.

All right, she thought. The chase is on!

Nancy quickly formulated her plan. A mile later she found the spot to execute it—another farm. The dirt yard surrounding the barn was even wetter than the one at the last farm. A tractor had gouged deep tracks in the mud, she could see. Thank goodness for the previous night's rain!

Quickly Nancy drove to the far side of the barnyard and turned right. Next, she pushed open her door and slumped down in her seat. From a distance, she hoped, it would look as if she had abandoned her car and run into the barn.

Twenty seconds later the engine of the other

car grew louder. As she had hoped, it immediately swung into the far side of the barnyard—the side that was the muddiest. With luck, the other car was now hubcap-deep in the mud. She heard its door close softly.

Nancy waited a few seconds longer, to give the driver time to get halfway to the barn. Then she sat up.

She wanted to check out the driver of the other car. One good look at his face was all she needed—

It wasn't a he. With a start, Nancy saw who it was.

Brenda!

The girl was trying to tiptoe gingerly through the mud. It wasn't going well. Her leather jacket, calf-length wool skirt, and expensive-looking boots just weren't right for the job. A grimace of disgust twisted her mouth as her right boot slid ankle-deep into the muck.

As she heard Nancy's door slam, she looked panicked and started back for her car. But her feet kept sinking.

Soon Brenda gave up. She stood still—and visibly sank deeper into the mud. "Nancy, you tricked me! I thought you were inside!" she yelled.

Nancy snapped open her door and climbed

out, trying hard not to smile. "Brenda, if you want leads for your stories, why not just phone?"

Brenda folded her arms. "Oh, sure, like you'd really help me!"

Nancy finally gave in to a grin. "Maybe I would, and maybe I wouldn't."

Brenda became indignant. "You can't stop me from reporting the news!"

Nancy shook her head. "I'm not 'news' and you know it. You're just hoping I'll do your thinking for you. Well, from now on you can do your own thinking, Brenda."

Brenda's jaw tightened. "I have. You're not the only girl in River Heights with a brain, you know. In fact, I even know who the insider at Hayward Security is."

Nancy was interested. Reaching inside her car, she switched off the ignition key. "Who is it?"

Brenda walked toward her, her boots making little sucking sounds in the mud. "I think it's Hayward's vice-president, Neil Masterson," she said. "If anyone can fiddle with the alarm systems, it's him. Plus he's got a motive," she hinted.

Now Nancy was *really* interested. "What motive?"

"His baby daughter."

Nancy recalled the photo on Neil's desk. What was the little girl's name? Tasha. She frowned. "What do you mean?"

Brenda finally drew near. "She has a congenital heart defect. She's had several operations. *Expensive* operations."

"So what? Neil's medical insurance pays for that," Nancy reasoned.

Brenda shook her head. "Only to a point. Most medical plans have a limit. I checked, and Neil has exceeded the Hayward plan's limit."

"Are you sure?" Nancy asked.

"Oh, yes. His little girl had three operations last year. We're talking about open-heart surgery, you understand. That adds up very fast. The total cost must have been hundreds of thousands of dollars."

There was no way that Neil Masterson could be making that kind of money. So how was he paying the hospital bills? Nancy would have to find out.

The corners of Brenda's mouth curled smugly. "So, what do you think? Is that excellent detective work, or what?"

Nancy shrugged. "Maybe, maybe not. Your father is a smart man. I know that, too."

Brenda recoiled as if stung. Bull's-eye, Nancy thought. It was her father who had found out about Masterson.

"Well, thanks for the tip," Nancy said, climbing back into her Mustang. "And good luck getting out of that mud."

"Aren't you going to help me?" Brenda wailed.

"You need a tractor. Or maybe a team of oxen," Nancy joked.

"Why, you—! Okay, I'll go find a farmer," Brenda said tightly. "But before you go, get this straight: I'm going to crack this case, Nancy Drew. And I don't need any help from you!"

As Nancy roared away, she shook her head in wonder. If Brenda truly wanted to catch the insider at Hayward Security, she wasn't going to do it by tailing a detective.

Nancy drove directly to Hayward's head-quarters. Neil Masterson was in a good mood when she was shown into his office.

They talked amiably for a few minutes. Then, having broken the ice, Nancy leaned back in her chair.

"By the way, I saw on your job application that you were in the army."

"Six years," he said proudly.

"Did you have any demolitions training while you were enlisted?" Nancy asked.

"Some—why?" His tone grew cautious.

"Just wondering. Tell me, do you watch the eleven o'clock news on TV?" she went on conversationally.

"No, my wife and I usually go to bed around ten."

Nancy said, "So you were at home with your wife last night?"

"All night. Why are you asking?" Neil was definitely suspicious now.

"Just—"

"Wondering, yes, I know," he finished. "Nancy, you're checking on my whereabouts, aren't you? Does this mean you suspect that *I* might be involved in the robberies?"

"I have to cover all possibilities," Nancy said hastily.

"Where I spend my free time is my business! I don't owe an explanation to you or anyone else!" His face was red with anger. "Now, if you'll excuse me, I have to see some people." Rising, he walked quickly out of his office.

Nancy was stunned. Why was Neil acting so guilty? If anything, she was more suspicious of him now than before.

Later that afternoon Cindy Larson arrived at Nancy's house. She was carrying a file folder. Her face was flushed with excitement.

"Hi," Nancy said, pulling a second chair over to her desk. "We're going to write a profile of Stanley Loomis today," Nancy announced.

"Good. I've already begun his," Cindy said.

"You have?"

Cindy grinned. "He acted so suspicious on Saturday yelling at Tom over that loudspeaker and all, so today on the way over I stopped at the library and looked him up in *Who's Who in River Heights*. The Chamber of Commerce publishes it. Then I searched the indexes for the city newspapers and found some real old articles about him."

"Anything interesting?" Nancy asked.

"He used to be a burglar," Cindy announced.

"What!"

Cindy nodded. "That was a long time ago. He went to prison and reformed—or so he said. After his parole he went into the security business. He told his customers that he could protect them better than anyone else because he knew better than anyone else how to rob them!"

"Quite a sales pitch," Nancy said dryly. "Good work, Cindy."

Cindy beamed. "Anything else?"

"We need to write a profile on Tom's vice-president, Neil Masterson," Nancy said.

"You're kidding! He lives across the street from me." Cindy sat down. "Nancy, I can't believe he's a suspect. He's so nice! I've even baby-sat his daughter, Tasha."

"Even so, we're starting a profile," Nancy said grimly. "Hold on! You say he lives right across the street?"

"Uh-huh." Cindy looked troubled.

"Can you see his garage and driveway clearly from your room?" Nancy asked.

"Yes."

Nancy tapped her pencil on her desktop. "Fantastic. Cindy, how would you like to do some surveillance?"

"I—I guess so," Cindy answered uncertainly.

"Good. Watch his house tonight. If he leaves, jot down the time. Also write down the time when he returns. Don't try to follow him anywhere, though. Just watch."

"Will this prove him innocent?" Cindy asked hopefully.

"I'm pretty sure the thieves'll be working tonight. If Neil is one of them, he'll go out. If he doesn't—well, it may not prove that he's innocent, necessarily, but it will help."

"I'll do it, then," Cindy promised. "Boy, it sure is creepy to suspect one of my own neighbors! I feel like a traitor."

"When you're a detective," Nancy said, "you have to ignore your personal feelings and be objective about everyone."

When Nancy went downstairs for dinner that evening, her father was waiting for her. She had a pretty good idea of what he wanted to talk to her about.

"I guess you saw my car, huh?" she asked in a small voice.

Carson nodded gravely. "I did. Would you like to tell me what happened?"

She told him.

Carson wearily rubbed his eyes. He was still in his business suit and looked tired. "Nancy, it isn't worth the risk."

"Yes, it is. Dad, listen—" Nancy began.

Her father cut her off with an angry wave of his hand. "No, *you* listen. I won't let you risk your life. This time you're up against professionals, Nancy—ruthless, violent men!"

"Yes, but . . ." Nancy's voice trailed off. She knew he was right.

"Nancy—" Carson's voice softened. "It looks to me like you're trying to prove something with this case. What? Does it have something to do with your young assistant?"

"With Cindy? No. What makes you think that?" Nancy asked, genuinely puzzled.

"I thought that maybe you were trying not to let her down—to be professional yourself. A professional detective, that is."

"No, that's not it—not exactly," Nancy said. The truth was, she hadn't felt that there was anything special about this case—until now. But now that her father had pointed it out, she realized that there *was* something different. She sighed. "I guess it started when I spoke at the Career Fair on Saturday. Remember that?"

"Uh-huh."

Nancy went on. "Well, I hadn't realized it until now, but it got me wondering about my own career—you know, what I'm going to do with my life. I want to know what it would be like to be a real detective—a full-time, *career* detective."

"So you decided to try it out?" Carson guessed.

Nancy nodded. "Sort of. You see, on this case I've tried to be totally professional. I've tried to treat Tom like a client."

A smile grew on her father's face. "I understand. But, sweetheart, remember you've got plenty of time to choose your career. Years, in fact. You don't have to rush."

"No, I don't suppose I do." Nancy smiled, too. In a way, she felt a whole lot better thinking that. "But, Dad, now that I've started this case, I have to finish it. I'm not a quitter. You taught me that." But would he let her continue her investigation? She held her breath while he thought.

"Okay, finish the job," Carson said after a minute. "But promise me something—"

Nancy hugged him. "Anything!"

"From now on take Bess or George with you when you patrol the warehouse district," he requested.

"I promise," Nancy said.

That night Nancy positioned herself on a platform high up the side of a grain silo near the river. She was bundled in a thick wool sweater and her leather jacket.

George was with her. "Tell me again why we're up here?" her friend asked.

"Because it's a good surveillance point. And because this time I can stay still and let the robbers do the moving around," Nancy explained. She reached into her knapsack.

To help her she had borrowed a piece of equipment from Chief McGinnis. It was a Night Vision Device—an NVD, for short. It had a lens like the zoom lens on a camera, a slim rectangular body, and a binocularlike eyepiece. By adjusting the brightness control on its side, she could turn night into a high-contrast, green-colored day.

It was cold and windy on the platform, but the view was perfect. Peering through the NVD, she began to survey the rooftops below. Most robberies, she knew, involved a lookout. Where better to station one than on a roof?

For more than an hour she scanned the area, moving methodically up and down the grid of streets. She was already familiar with most of the buildings. From this angle, though, they looked vulnerable. Many had easy points of entry on their roofs.

Then Nancy caught a sudden movement. Swinging the NVD back, she searched a rooftop half a block away.

There!

She caught the movement again. By the

stairwell door. She focused. Nancy was looking at a hideous face. Its skin was rotted and blackened. Teeth and jawbone showed through a ragged hole in its cheek. Dried blood caked its empty eye sockets.

Then the face turned. Pupils shone from deep in the bloody sockets. It was staring right at her.

Chapter
Nine

Nancy gasped. Her heart began to pound. Then she forced herself to think rationally. Dead men did not move around. It was a rubber Halloween mask on a robber. And she was sure he couldn't see her in the dark.

"Nan, what's wrong?" George asked, but Nancy just waved her to silence.

Nancy continued to follow him as he looked over the edge of the roof. After scanning slowly right and left, he waved his arm. It was a signal—*all clear.*

The thieves were about to strike! Nancy

repacked her knapsack and tore down the ladder to the street, George close behind.

When they reached the street, Nancy tossed her keys to George. "Start the car and wait here. Keep the passenger door open. I may need to get in in a hurry."

"Where are you going?" George asked.

"Just to verify there's a robbery in progress. As soon as I'm sure, I'll be right back—then we'll drive to a phone."

It took only a minute to reach the corner of the building. She crouched low and risked a peek. No trucks, no robbers, no open loading bays. Everything was shut tight. What was going on? Nancy slid around the corner and started down the street, hugging the wall and darting between shadows.

Except for her, there was no movement at all on the block.

Suddenly forty yards ahead of her a door flew open. A figure darted out and ran down the street at top speed. Nancy could plainly see the rubber mask pulled over his head. It was him!

She took off. Her knapsack made running awkward, so she shucked it off and tossed it into a shadow. She would get it later. Right now it was more important to follow the Dead Man.

The chase lasted for five blocks. It was the same guy she had chased two nights earlier, Nancy realized excitedly. She recognized the way he pumped his arms and lifted his knees. Track athletes ran that way. She saw that she was falling behind. Rats! She *couldn't* lose him—not now! She speeded up.

Then, halfway up the hill, Nancy saw a swirling red light bouncing off the buildings ahead. A police car was around the corner! The Dead Man saw it, too, and quickly darted down an alley. When Nancy reached it, she saw him sprinting up a fire escape to a roof above.

She decided not to follow. He was trapped, she knew. Catching him would only be a matter of surrounding the building and tightening the net. She ran to the corner to flag the approaching police car.

There were three of them speeding toward her. Nancy skidded halfway into the street and began to wave her arms. The first two whizzed by her at high speed. The third screeched to a stop. Chief McGinnis was in the passenger seat. He rolled down his window and shouted,

"Nancy, get in! There's a five-five-oh at Up-town Electronics."

"No! It's back at All-County, and one of the guys is on the roof of that building!" She pointed. "I chased him there!"

"What?"

Rapidly Nancy explained. The chief ordered his driver to dispatch four cars to trap the Dead Man. Satisfied, Nancy climbed in the backseat.

"But, Chief, I thought we were going to All-County Moving and Storage!" Nancy said as they pulled up in front of Uptown Electronics. "I saw the lookout signal an all-clear from that roof."

"I'm afraid you're mistaken, Nancy—see?" the chief said.

A pair of medics was wheeling out a stretcher. Strapped to it was a young man in a Hayward Security uniform.

"I don't understand," Nancy muttered. "This doesn't make sense, unless—"

"Unless what?" the chief asked.

"The lookout wasn't a lookout at all, but a decoy," she said dejectedly.

After Nancy returned with George, they quickly learned the facts. The gang had keyed off the alarm, grabbed the guard, knocked him out, and made their getaway with fifty thousand dollars' worth of laptop computers. The police had been called by the guard after he came to.

The chief's men had not found the decoy. The man was obviously familiar with the area and had an escape route ready. Nancy felt terribly frustrated.

Nancy turned to Tom and the chief. "The laptop computers they took were worth a lot, but they could easily have taken more. They took only twenty-five boxes."

"It's almost as if they're robbing for the sport of it," George remarked.

The chief shrugged. "Usually profit is the motive behind a robbery."

Nancy excused herself to call Cindy Larson. It was late, but Cindy was still awake, watching out her bedroom window.

"Mr. Masterson came home at six o'clock and he's been inside ever since," Cindy reported with obvious relief.

"Okay, thanks. I'll see you tomorrow after school," Nancy said. "Oh, and Cindy—wear old clothes that you don't care about."

"Why?" Her assistant was curious.

"It's probably better if I don't tell you. See you then."

Nancy hung up and bit her lip thoughtfully. That Neil Masterson had an alibi didn't completely clear him, she knew. But it helped.

The following morning Nancy called Neil Masterson's office and found that Adam Reeves had not been on duty the night before.

Checking Stanley Loomis's whereabouts was even easier. The business section of *Today's Times* carried an article describing a speech he had given to the River Heights Retail Merchants Association the night before. In it he had stressed the need for reliable security. The alibi didn't clear him, but it did indicate he couldn't have taken part in the robbery.

Next she phoned Chief McGinnis to ask if there had been any sign of the stolen goods. The chief told her nothing had surfaced.

Nancy spent the rest of the morning focusing on the profiles of her three strongest suspects.

She went to check out Adam Reeves's apartment building. It was clean and well maintained. Not fancy, but nice. The refuse area behind the building was orderly. She had no trouble finding what she needed. After loading it in her trunk, she drove home.

She was studying Adam Reeves's credit report when Cindy arrived.

"So soon?" her assistant asked, pulling over her seat. "I thought it would take weeks for that to get here."

"I asked them to fax it to my father's office," Nancy told her.

"What does it tell us?" Cindy asked.

"Plenty. When you add up everything he's spending, it totals up to more than he's making."

"Where does he get the extra money?" Cindy wondered.

"Good question. This credit report lists only one employer, so it's a pretty good bet that he hasn't got a second job," Nancy said.

They went to the garage then, and Nancy backed out her car so they'd have plenty of room to work. After opening her trunk, she lifted out the plastic garbage bag she had taken from Adam's garbage can.

Cindy gulped. "Nancy, are we going to do what I think we're going to do?"

"Uh-huh," Nancy confirmed, spreading newspapers on the driveway. "That's why I asked you to wear old clothes."

They both donned gardening gloves, and Nancy slashed open the bag.

"Oh, gross!" Cindy said, her face twisted in disgust.

"Dig in." Nancy smiled. "We need to make a list of everything we find."

When it was done, the list was quite revealing. Adam dined on sirloin, and liked expensive cologne. The most interesting discovery, though, were several copies of a magazine for entrepreneurs.

"It could be that Adam is planning to open a business," Nancy surmised.

"How can he do that if he's spending more than he makes?" Cindy wondered.

"He may be expecting to get a big lump of money soon," Nancy explained. "Now, let's review. Both Neil Masterson and Stanley Loomis could have masterminded these robberies," she summarized. "They both have the expertise, and they both have motives. Stanley Loomis wants to hurt his competition—Neil Masterson has hospital bills to pay."

"But what about all the money Adam Reeves is spending?" Cindy asked.

"If you ask me, he is the strongest suspect," Nancy said. "He had more opportunities than the others to be involved."

"So where do we go from here?" Cindy asked.

"You go back to the telephone," Nancy said. "A line on those stolen goods would help a lot. I'm going to do something I should have done two days ago."

"What's that?"

"Tail Adam Reeves," Nancy declared.

Adam left work at five o'clock. From the warehouse he drove to his apartment building. Nancy followed at a discreet distance. Parking down the street from his building, she watched him go inside. Then she settled down to wait.

At ten minutes after six Adam returned to his car. He had changed from his uniform into a suit and topcoat. He looked sharp.

To Nancy's surprise, he then went to a house several streets from hers, where he picked up a date: an attractive blond girl.

They went to Chez Louis, an expensive waterside restaurant. Nancy went in and sat at the bar and sipped a soda—slowly. She secretly kept her eyes focused on Adam's table. The girl looked utterly bored.

At least, she did until Adam presented her with a long, flat box from a jewelry store. Her face lit up, and she opened it with a cry of delight that Nancy could hear all the way at the bar. Inside was a gold necklace.

Nancy had seen enough. This reinforced her conclusion that Adam was living beyond his means. In fact, she now had enough evidence to confront him. And once confronted with some hard facts, he might make a confession.

If he didn't, he would nevertheless feel the pressure, and crooks under pressure tended to make mistakes.

Nancy walked to the parking lot and unlocked the door of her car. As she was bending down to get in, she was suddenly jerked up and off her feet.

She was caught from behind in a choke hold!

Chapter

Ten

NANCY COULDN'T BREATHE. She struggled, but it was pointless. The arm around her throat was like steel. She managed to squeeze out the words, *"Put . . . me . . . down!"*

"Not until you say why you're following me." The voice belonged to Adam Reeves.

"I can't—*aagh!*—breathe!"

Adam relaxed his grip. Nancy's toes met the ground, but he didn't let her go. She gulped in air. What should she say? If she blew it, Adam might kill her on the spot.

She decided to stick to the truth—part of it, anyway. "You worked at two of the warehouses that got robbed. Of course I'm following you —what did you expect?"

"Standard procedure, huh?" Adam mocked. He tightened his grip a notch. "You'll have to do better, Nancy."

"Okay." Nancy's windpipe hurt. She recited some facts. "You've got high balances on your credit cards. Your car payments are six hundred and forty-six dollars a month. You're planning to open a business, but you've got nothing in the bank. Get the idea?"

Adam suddenly released her, and Nancy slumped to the ground, gasping. But in a moment she was back on her feet and facing him with a cold stare.

"How do you know that stuff?" he demanded.

It was amazing how easily you could put someone off balance with a little research and intuition.

"Never mind how I know," she said, sounding more assertive than she felt. "You're in a lot of trouble, Adam."

"Baloney. That's not what *he* says."

"He?"

Adam caught himself. "Never mind who. Get to the point."

"The point is, my evidence shows that you're involved in something illegal. You'd better start cooperating."

Adam sneered. "You don't have anything solid on me."

Nancy was stuck. He was right. Surprising a confession out of him depended upon convincing him that she knew the whole story. But she didn't. Worried, she tried a new tack.

"Okay, Adam, I'll go easy. Just tell me where you did time." She mentally crossed her fingers.

Adam staggered back a step, as if struck. Nancy couldn't believe her luck. She had guessed right. A little more pressure and he might confess!

"You've done crimes before. And that choke hold—it's a mugger's move. Was that your game?"

"No! I—" Once more he stopped himself. He had amazing composure, Nancy realized in dismay. "You can't prove any of this."

Not yet, she couldn't. But she thought she knew how to. If only she could get his fingerprints.

Her eyes still locked on Adam's, Nancy reached behind her and began to open her car door.

Adam's hand shot out and shoved the door closed.

"Hey!" he growled. "I'm not done with you yet."

"Sorry," Nancy said sarcastically. "Look, since we aren't getting anywhere with this conversation, let's drop it."

For a moment Adam didn't move. Nancy was afraid he would grab her again, but he must have decided against it. Perhaps, she thought, he was remembering his date in the restaurant. What would she think if she was watching? With a hostile glare, he brushed past her and went back inside.

Nancy breathed a sigh of relief and got into her car. She wanted to get out of there—fast!

At home she immediately dusted the door of her car with a fine black powder.

"Nice fingerprints!" Chief McGinnis complimented her the next morning. "Almost a complete set, too. Where'd you get them?"

"From the door of my car," Nancy explained.

"Let's run 'em through the computer and see what turns up," the chief said.

Fifteen minutes later an officer came in with a manila folder. The chief opened it, scanned the contents, then handed it to Nancy.

"Well," she said when she had looked it over, "that explains where Adam disappeared to for six months. If you'll excuse me, Chief, I think I'll have a little talk with Tom Hayward about this."

"Prison?" Tom Hayward said, astonished. "A Hayward guard?"

"For grand larceny," Nancy affirmed. "Adam stole a car."

Tom shook his head. "But how can this be? We screen our employees thoroughly. We check for things like this. They take lie detector tests."

"An experienced liar can beat the detector," Nancy pointed out.

"But not that easily," Tom replied. "There's usually enough doubt about the results to disqualify the candidate."

"So how did Adam slip through?" Nancy wondered.

"That's what I'm going to find out," Tom

resolved. "It may take some doing, though. Adam was hired more than a year ago."

"Anything you find out will be a help," Nancy told him.

Tom tossed the fingerprint report onto the broad expanse of his glass-topped desk. His office was very large. Its corner windows overlooked green countryside and a man-made pond. In the pond a powerful waterjet shot an arc of water high into the air. Rainbow hues danced in the mist.

"I'll have to fire Adam, of course," Tom said.

"Wouldn't you rather leave him on duty so you can keep track of him?" Nancy suggested.

Tom brightened. "Good idea. We'll keep him off the streets."

"McGinnis will blanket the area with patrols tonight, right?" Tom inquired.

Nancy replied, "Yes, and I'll be watching our three main suspects."

"Three at once? How?" Tom wondered.

"Adam will be on duty at the CD warehouse," Nancy said. "My assistant has Neil Masterson's house under observation. That's two. As for Stanley Loomis, I'll follow him myself."

"I'm going with you," Tom announced.

Nancy was surprised. "You don't have to. I can cover him—with the help of some friends, of course."

"I believe you, but even so, I'm going. I'm tired of sitting around waiting for the next robbery to happen," Tom said with conviction. "I need to get involved."

"Fine with me," Nancy agreed. "It means I can give my friends Bess and George the night off. I'll pick you up here at sundown. Wear dark clothes in case we wind up on foot."

"No problem."

Just then the phone on Tom's desk trilled. He snatched up the handset. "Yes?" A pause. "Okay, put him on—"

The conversation lasted only a minute, but it was long enough to propel Tom out of his plush leather desk chair. He paced back and forth behind his desk, a worried look on his face. Concerned, Nancy watched as the phone cord stretched to its limit.

"Yeah . . . yeah . . . Can't you? No . . . okay . . . I see. Well, keep me informed."

Hanging up, he sank back into his chair with a weary sigh.

"Bad news?" Nancy asked.

"The worst," Tom said. "That was our banker in Chicago. The price of Hayward

Security stock has dropped another three and a half points. I have now lost three quarters of a million bucks. In one week."

"I'm sorry," Nancy said, stunned. "Let's hope we get some positive results tonight."

Nancy spent the rest of the day filling in the details on Adam Reeves. She read the court records of his trial, interviewed his neighbors, and phoned his ex-boss at the gas station. She found nothing unusual, though.

That evening she picked up Tom as arranged. Nancy got the feeling that he was itching for some action. He was tense and likely to be disappointed, she knew. For the most part surveillance was a passive activity.

Stanley Loomis worked late. At eight o'clock he drove to a steak house. At eight fifty-five he stopped at a video store and rented a movie. Then he drove home.

Nancy and Tom watched his house from her car for another hour or so. The lights were off except in the living room, where the bluish flicker of the TV could be seen through the window. At ten forty-five the lights went out. All was quiet.

"There's nothing happening here," Tom

said after a few more minutes. "Let's head down to the warehouse district."

"Fine by me," Nancy said. "We can check with the chief."

The warehouse district was quiet, too, according to the officers in a police car they stopped. Tom was impatient.

"They're around here somewhere. I can feel it!" he exclaimed, hitting Nancy's dashboard with his fist. "What do you say we check under the Interstate bridge?" Tom said.

"That's almost out of the district. There's nothing in that area except some scrap metal yards," Nancy countered.

"Exactly. See, I figure the gang hangs out somewhere near the warehouse district, not in it. They wait until they're sure the 'heat' has cooled, and then they move in."

"Sure," Nancy agreed, looking at Tom with increased respect. He was very sharp! "Why didn't I think of that? Let's go."

From a distance the bridge was a graceful, looping M outlined in lights. Up close it was a soaring steel dinosaur lumbering into the river on colossal concrete legs. Nancy coasted slowly through the wasteland that lay under the span. Wrecked cars and garbage were strewn about.

On the far side was a collection of auto salvagers, concrete mixing plants, and scrapyards. Twisted chain link fences wandered along the roadside.

"Looks deserted," Nancy remarked uneasily.

"Maybe, maybe not. Let's drive around," Tom suggested.

Yellow anticrime lights turned the area into something from a nightmare. Nancy turned left near a scrap metal yard.

"There! See him?" Tom exclaimed suddenly, pointing.

Nancy snapped her head around. Leaning against a chain link fence near the open gateway to the scrapyard was a figure in black. A rubber Wolfman mask was pulled over his head.

"Yes!" Nancy twisted the wheel and swung toward him. As her headlights swept over him, the Wolfman darted inside the yard. Strange, she thought. Hadn't he seen them approaching sooner?

"Let's go!" Tom said. "We can catch him!"

"Shouldn't we call—"

"There are two of us. We can corner him!" Tom had his door open already. As Nancy braked to a halt, he leaped out and dashed into the yard in pursuit of the Wolfman.

Nancy grabbed her keys and followed. She was worried. Tom was taking a terrible risk.

On the other hand they now had one of the robbers cornered. The chain link fence was twelve feet high and topped with barbed wire. No way was the Wolfman going anywhere. This was their best break yet, she knew.

Inside, she looked around. There was no sign of either Tom or their prey. Which direction should she go?

"Nancy! Up on the scaffolding!" Tom called from somewhere nearby.

She turned toward the scrapyard's office building. It was an old wooden structure two stories high. Metal scaffolding enveloped it. Then she saw the Wolfman darting up a ladder.

"I see him!" she called.

Nancy raced to the ladder. Should she follow? She looked around. Still no sign of Tom. He was probably on the opposite side of the building, she realized, closing in on the Wolfman from the other direction.

She decided to risk it. This time she was not facing her adversary alone. Nimbly she sped up the ladder. No Wolfman. She scrambled up another ladder and found herself on the roof. The stairwell enclosure in the middle of the roof provided the only cover. The Wolfman had to be hiding behind it!

Nancy's heart was pounding. Quietly she tiptoed to the edge of the roof and looked down. On the ground two stories below her was a collection of scrap metal. Razor-sharp edges glinted in the half light.

"Tom?" she called. Where was he?

Suddenly two hands smashed into her back. With a scream, she went hurtling off the platform toward the jagged metal below!

Chapter

Eleven

As NANCY FELL, a picture of her father flashed into her mind. He's going to be furious with me, she thought.

Then her fall was broken against a pair of strong arms, and she slid easily to the ground. It took her a moment to realize that she wasn't dead.

"I—I can't believe you were standing here!" she said to Tom. Another few inches and she would have been sliced to ribbons by the scrap metal.

He was amazingly calm. He said, "It's a lucky thing I was!"

"Thank you. I thought you were up on the scaffolding, too!"

She wanted to stay right there with his arms around her for a few minutes, but a troubling thought had struck her. "The guy in the wolf mask is still up on the roof."

"You're right," Tom agreed. "Look, we'd better call the police."

She raked back her hair with her fingers. "You don't want to trap him anymore?"

"Not after what just happened to you."

Before they were halfway to her Mustang, they heard an engine roar to life. A second later a low-slung car shot around the corner of the building.

"Look out!" Nancy yelled. Grabbing Tom, she pulled him out of the way. Together they tumbled to the ground.

The car shot past them and sped through the gate. Its lights were off, including the license plate bulb, so Nancy missed the number. She sprang to her feet, but by the time she had run into the street, the car was turning a distant corner. She saw its lights snap on as it did.

"Rats!"

Tom ran up next to her. "I didn't get the number, did you?"

"No!" she said in frustration. "I can't even say for sure what model it is."

"Maybe we can catch it?"

"Doubtful," Nancy predicted.

Tom shrugged. "At least we got close."

Nancy was suddenly angry. Stalking toward her car, she muttered, "Close isn't good enough, Tom. Not for me."

The first thing Nancy did upon arriving home half an hour later was to confirm the whereabouts of her suspects. She phoned Cindy.

"I hope I'm not calling too late," she said apologetically.

"No problem, but I don't have any news," Cindy reported. "Mr. Masterson has been home since a quarter past six."

Nancy thanked her and hung up. Next she dialed the nighttime number at Hayward Security headquarters. Guards were required to phone in every hour to confirm that they were on duty and awake. If they failed to report in, then headquarters dispatched a van to check on them.

The switchboard operator told Nancy that Adam Reeves had phoned in every hour.

"You spoke to him personally?" Nancy asked, to be certain.

"Sure. Well, sort of. The guards usually don't say much," the operator explained. "They give their ID number, say 'Reporting in,' and then hang up."

"Well, thanks a lot for your help."

Stanley Loomis was also a suspect, but she was positive that he had not been at the scene. He couldn't have left his house and driven to the area faster than she and Tom. Also, the Wolfman had been tall and agile. Loomis was short and fat. Still, that didn't put him completely in the clear. This gang had more than one member, and some of them might work for Loomis.

The next morning Nancy drove to Loomis's main office. Like Tom, Loomis had a fleet of vans, she saw. He had more than Tom did, in fact.

That meant he employed a lot of guards. Nancy needed to find out more about them. She went to one of the cafeterias in the warehouse district that was popular with workers.

It was nearly empty. The cashier was reading a paperback. Nancy asked for a pack of

gum. As she paid for it, she said, "Can I ask
you a question or two?"

"What for?" the cashier asked warily, hand-
ing Nancy her change.

"My name's Nancy Drew," Nancy began.

The woman's face lit up. "Haven't I seen
your name in the paper? Aren't you the girl
detective they're always writing about?"

"That's right," Nancy confirmed. "And I'm
trying to help a friend."

"What do you want to know?" the woman
asked, smiling.

"Warehouse workers eat here a lot, right?"
Nancy asked.

"They're our main customers," the cashier
affirmed.

"Do the security guards ever come in, too?"

"Sometimes."

Nancy nodded encouragingly. "Do they ever
talk about the companies they work for? Do
they ever complain?"

The cashier laughed. "Nancy, every worker
complains!"

"What about the security guards, though?"
Nancy persisted.

"Why don't you ask that guy over there."
The cashier pointed.

"Thanks," Nancy said.

The man was in his late forties and had a ruddy complexion. He was drinking coffee at a Formica-topped table by the window. Although he wasn't wearing a uniform, a Loomis & Petersen jacket was hanging over the back of his chair.

A newspaper was open in front of him. He was reading the want ads, Nancy saw. "Excuse me, may I ask you a few questions?"

"What for?" the man inquired without looking up.

Nancy ran through the same routine that she had with the cashier. Satisfied, the man offered her the seat across the table.

"Thanks," Nancy said, sitting. "You work for Stan Loomis?"

"Not anymore," the man said glumly. "Laid off a week ago."

Nancy lifted her eyebrows. "Why?"

"Things are tough everywhere, I guess," the man replied. "Company had to tighten its belt."

"Gee, I'm sorry. How long did you work for him?" Nancy asked sympathetically.

"Seventeen years! Still can't believe it," the man muttered.

Nancy leaned toward him. "You must be pretty angry."

"Well, I'd rather somebody else got laid off than me, I'll say that," the man grumbled.

Nancy zeroed in on her target. "Would you say Stan Loomis is honest?"

"Sure," the man said without hesitation. "Stan was on the wrong side of the law once. He told me all about it. But he reformed. He's as honest as my mother—and believe me, kid, that's honest!"

Nancy smiled. "I believe you. What about Hayward Security—think you might get a job working for them?"

"Wouldn't want it," the man said firmly.

"Why not?" Nancy was surprised.

"'Cause I've talked to their guards. The pay's lousy."

"Any other reasons?" Nancy asked.

The man stirred his coffee thoughtfully. "Not that I can put my finger on. The guys who work there are kind of—I don't know, unhappy. They don't have a lot of nice things to say about the company, you get my drift?"

"I think so. And thanks," Nancy said, rising. "You've been a big help."

* * *

When Cindy Larson arrived at Nancy's house that afternoon, she asked, "What can I do to help?"

Nancy slid the telephone toward her. "You can call more discount stores. I've listed numbers from the rest of the county. That will free me up to work on our profiles."

Cindy's face fell. "But I've called so many already! Isn't there something else I can do?"

"Getting bored?" Nancy asked with a smile.

"Well, a little," Cindy admitted sheepishly.

"Don't get discouraged. You never know when a clue will turn up."

"I suppose." Cindy reached for the phone.

Suddenly Nancy felt guilty. She placed her hand on Cindy's to stop her from dialing. "Actually, there *is* something else you could help me with—"

"Not more garbage, I hope?" Cindy groaned.

Nancy shook her head. "No. What time is the mail delivered in your neighborhood?"

Cindy looked at her watch. "Right about now."

"Does Neil Masterson's wife get it out of the mailbox?"

"No, Mr. Masterson does that when he gets

home from work. At least, that's what I saw him do the last couple of evenings."

"Good enough," Nancy said, rising from her chair. "Let's go."

They drove to Cindy's neighborhood. It was a new development—mostly ranch-style houses.

They cruised up and down the block several times, checking to see that no one was in Neil's yard. Then Nancy quickly pulled up to the curbside mailbox and took his mail.

"Nancy, isn't opening other people's mail illegal?" Cindy asked, aghast. She looked a bit pale, Nancy saw.

"We're not going to open it," Nancy said, driving away.

"Then why steal it?"

"We're not stealing it. We're borrowing it," she said.

"Now I'm *really* confused! Why borrow it if—"

"I'll show you why in a minute."

Back in her bedroom, Nancy opened her windows wide. Next, she sorted through Neil's mail. There was some junk mail and also what appeared to be a bill from River Heights Hospital.

In addition, there was an envelope from Loomis & Petersen. Interesting. Nancy put it and the hospital bill in the center of her desk. Then she went to her closet and took out a bottle of clear fluid. "This is highly flammable," she warned.

Using an eyedropper, Nancy dribbled some of the fluid on the envelope from River Heights Hospital. Instantly the wet part of the envelope became transparent.

As Nancy had suspected, it was a bill. The amount due was $5,425. A very hefty sum. Nancy blew on the wet spot. Within a minute the envelope was once again opaque.

"That's incredible," Cindy said, shaking her head.

Next Nancy dribbled fluid onto the envelope from Loomis & Petersen. Her eyes went wide. Inside was a check made out to Neil Masterson. The amount it paid him was exactly $5,425!

Chapter
Twelve

THAT EXPLAINED how Neil was able to pay the bills for his daughter's operations. But what did Loomis get in exchange? Information about Hayward's alarm systems? Access codes?

Or was it more than that? And what about Adam Reeves? Where did he fit in? In an unguarded moment Adam had mentioned a "he." Who was that? Neil? Loomis?

Nancy needed definite answers. Time was running out. The price of Hayward Security stock had dropped even farther that day. Tom and his shareholders were losing a fortune. She had to get to the bottom of things, and fast. It was time, Nancy decided, to call in her reserves.

Bess and George arrived at Nancy's right after dinner. Cindy stayed, too. The four parked themselves in Nancy's room.

"Starting tonight we have to keep a constant tail on Loomis, Masterson, and Reeves," she announced. "We want to know everything they do, everyone they meet."

"Okay!" Bess said. "Exactly what do we have to do?"

"Borrow your parents' cars, pick up your target, and stick with him. Keep a record of everything: locations, times—the works. George, you take Adam Reeves. But be careful. He can spot a tail."

"If he spots me, at least I'll have a shot at outrunning him," George joked.

Nancy warned, "Stay in your car. If he sees you, take off."

"Who do I get?" Bess asked.

"Neil Masterson," Nancy told her.

"Is he cute?"

The others howled in mock outrage and threw pillows at her.

"Hey! My hair!" Bess wailed. When the melee died down, she added, "I guess that leaves you with Loomis, Nancy."

"What about me?" Cindy asked.

"We need you to be our central contact. If there are any problems, we'll call in to you, and you can get word to one or both of the others."

"I just sit by the phone?" Cindy looked disappointed.

"You are our lifeline," Nancy told her seriously. "That's important."

That's dull, Cindy's expression said. But she only nodded.

"Okay, let's get going. We'll stick with our targets until they go home. Then we'll pick them up again in the morning," Nancy said.

That night was a washout. Adam worked at the CD warehouse, then drove straight home. Neil worked late, then went home, too, leaving Bess to spend the evening parked by Cindy's house while Cindy spent the evening by Nancy's phone.

Nancy herself traveled a bit more, but in the

end Stanley Loomis did nothing very unusual. His one unexpected stop was at a florist, where he walked out with a dozen pink tulips. He took them home. Nancy realized for the first time that he was probably married.

Saturday morning the team was at work early. Nancy was still sipping tea from her thermos when Loomis climbed into his car and drove to his office.

Nancy parked halfway down the block from his office—close enough to see him leave, far enough not to be noticed. Then she settled in for a long wait.

Tap, tap, tap.

The rapping on her window caught her completely off guard.

"Bess!" She rolled down her window. "What are you doing here?"

Bess grinned. "Same thing you are. I just parked a little farther way, that's all. When I saw your car I came over."

Nancy jerked herself upright. "But that must mean that Neil Masterson is—"

"You got it." Bess nodded. "He arrived at Loomis's office a few minutes ago. Do you think they're inside having some kind of pow-wow?"

"I'd lay odds on it," Nancy said. Reaching behind her, she got her knapsack. Inside the pack were her binoculars and a camera with a telephoto lens. "Let's go."

"Where?"

"Where we can see into Loomis's office. We should have a couple of rooftops to choose from."

"Rooftops?" Bess echoed nervously.

The building Nancy chose was diagonally across the street from Loomis & Petersen. In an alley next to it she leaped up and caught the lowest rung of the fire escape.

"But, Nancy—" Bess said in a worried voice.

"You can stay here if you like," Nancy pointed out.

Bess looked around the alley. "No, thanks. I'll go with you."

A minute later they were in position. A rooftop sign hid them. By peering with her binoculars through a gap in the sign, Nancy could see directly into Loomis's office without being detected. Neil Masterson was indeed meeting with Loomis.

"What are they doing?" Bess asked.

"Looking at some diagrams," Nancy reported. "Neil is pointing things out with his pen. Loomis likes what he sees."

"What are they planning, I wonder?" Bess mused.

Nancy shook her head. "I don't know, but I'm pretty sure of one thing—Tom Hayward knows nothing about this."

That night Nancy switched places with George to tail Adam Reeves. Saturday night was a prime time for robbery since the warehouse district would be all but deserted. Since Adam was the suspect most likely to be part of an actual strike, she wanted to be the one covering him.

According to his work schedule, Adam was off. When he left his apartment, he was dressed all in black. Nancy's excitement grew as she followed him downtown because he doubled back a few times, obviously checking for a tail. Nancy countered his moves perfectly.

There was no moon that night. Nancy snapped off her headlights and used only the light from the streetlights. Adam finally parked in the warehouse district. Nancy did, too.

Finally, close to midnight, a van came up their street from the direction of the river. Adam started his car and followed it around the corner. Her pulse quickening, Nancy got out and followed on foot.

Adam's destination was an audio components warehouse. She had passed it many times on her earlier patrols. As she watched from the shadows thirty yards away, Adam got out of his car—only now he wore the Wolfman mask. Nancy snapped a picture.

The van backed up to the loading bay. Another figure dressed in black got out of it—the Dead Man. Nancy recognized the grisly mask instantly. She took another shot.

The two men opened the back doors of the van and wheeled out handcarts. The Dead Man went to the alarm system keypad and pushed a sequence of keys. The red light that had been blinking on the panel went off. They rolled up the door.

As Nancy had expected, they worked mostly in the dark, using flashlights. They were fast, too. She saw them zoom between the warehouse and the van twice in less than a minute.

Nancy crept closer. She wanted to get as much on film as possible.

The Wolfman and the Dead Man disappeared inside the warehouse for more than a minute. Nancy crept closer. There was no sign of them.

She was now close enough to make out the lettering on the van. It said, "Hayward Security Systems." No wonder no one ever noticed them coming or going! They had the perfect camouflage: a vehicle that was totally familiar to people in the district. And to the police. And to her.

Was it a fake Hayward van or the real thing?

Nancy darted up to the loading bay. The thieves were now deep inside the warehouse.

She leaped up onto the loading platform because she needed a picture of the interior of the van, and that was the only way she could get it. She sighted through the viewfinder.

No good. She moved back, stepping carefully around a small aluminum ladder that someone had left set up inside the warehouse. She sighed again—still no good.

When she was twenty feet away she sighted again. Perfect. Then, through the viewfinder, she saw the aluminum ladder come into the picture. It was falling! It clattered onto the platform. Nancy froze.

She peered into the darkness and saw who had knocked the ladder over. *Cindy!*

"I'm sorry!" Cindy whispered.

"What are you doing here?" Nancy whispered back, furious.

"I—I wanted to get in on the excitement," Cindy replied, "so I followed you down here."

This was no time to lecture the girl, Nancy knew. "Let's get out of here before—"

It was too late. From inside the warehouse Nancy heard the sound of running feet. The Wolfman and the Dead Man were coming!

Chapter
Thirteen

INSTEAD OF RUNNING down the street, Nancy grabbed Cindy and hauled her into the warehouse to fake out the robbers. Boxes of stereo parts were stacked on top of wooden pallets. The pallets were arranged in long parallel rows running from the front of the warehouse to the back.

Nancy yanked Cindy down the aisle that was closest to the right wall. The thieves weren't likely to come that way—she hoped.

When they reached the back wall, they found an aisle perpendicular to the others.

Nancy pulled Cindy behind the last pallet of components. Now they were no longer visible from the front of the warehouse.

Nancy heard the thieves run up to the loading bay door. A second later powerful flashlight beams shone down the aisles. Bright circles of light played against the wall to either side of them. The stack of boxes hid them, but Nancy knew that the thieves must suspect someone was there.

Nancy put her mouth to Cindy's ear and whispered, *"Don't move!"*

The warning was hardly necessary. Cindy was nearly frozen with terror.

Nancy looked around for a makeshift weapon. There was nothing within reach. Naturally, *this* warehouse would be spotless! The only thing available was her camera. Nancy was surprised, somehow, that she still had it in her hand. Too bad the flash attachment wasn't on. She might have been able to blind them temporarily.

Male voices conferred near the front. Then Nancy heard the van's rear doors slam. Hope seized her. Were they leaving?

Not right away, it turned out. The next sound she heard was that of a tool working on a pipe—a pipe wrench? What were they doing? After a minute, a loud clanging began. They were hammering on a pipe. Why?

The loading bay door rolled down and was locked, leaving them in total darkness. There was the muffled sound of the van starting up, and then the engine fading in the distance. They were alone. Nancy whipped a penlight from her pocket, switched it on, and grabbed Cindy's hand.

"Let's get out of here!"

As they drew close to the front, Nancy stopped—and sniffed. There was an odor in the air.

"Gas! That's what they did! They ruptured a gas line!"

"W-we're going to d-die," Cindy whimpered.

"No, we're not, but we'd better get out of here soon," Nancy cautioned.

The loading bay door couldn't be opened. The control panel inside was identical to the one outside. The code had to be keyed in. A door in the office led out, too, but it was locked. Nancy searched the office for a key, but couldn't find one. She tried the phones. Dead.

"The wires outside were cut," she guessed.

Nancy found the light switches and flicked

them until the warehouse interior was completely lit. Then she raced to find the gas leak.

"Help me trace this line!" she ordered Cindy. "Maybe we can find a valve that will turn it off." But there wasn't one. If there was, it was on the outside.

The smell of gas was now heavy in the air. Nancy felt dizzy. How long would it take the warehouse to completely fill with gas? An hour? Fifteen minutes? She forced herself to think.

"An emergency exit! There has to be one!"

There was, set into the back wall. But it was chained shut.

"That's illegal!" Nancy fumed.

Nancy ran along the back wall, looking up. Yes! About ten feet up on the wall was a row of three lateral windows. They were too high up to reach with the aluminum ladder.

"We've got to build a pyramid out of boxes," she said urgently.

They began to move the stereo components, erecting a crude cardboard stairway. It was growing increasingly difficult to work, however. The smell of the gas was overpowering. Nancy felt like gagging. Cindy began to cough. They had to get out—soon!

At last they reached the windows, but the handles on them wouldn't budge. They were rusted in place. They would have to break the windows open, but with what?

"The ladder!" Nancy said.

The trip for the ladder was agonizing. The gas stung Nancy's throat and eyes. Returning to the rear wall, she gripped the ladder by two middle rungs, climbed up the cardboard stairway, and thrust the ladder against the window.

It bounced off. She tried again. This time, the window cracked.

"Hurry!" Cindy urged, her voice a series of choking coughs.

Two more thrusts and cool, fresh air was pouring in through a hole. A minute later the glass was completely out. Nancy cried in triumph, "We did it!"

She helped Cindy out first. Then she squirmed through the narrow space and dropped ten feet into the alley outside.

"N-Nancy, I'm so sorry! I almost got us killed," her assistant sobbed.

Nancy hugged her. "Cindy, it's okay. We got out. That's all that counts. Come on, let's call the police and the fire department."

* * *

As she slept that night, Nancy dreamed that she was choking. In the morning she barely touched her breakfast.

Later, in her bathroom, she developed the pictures she had taken the night before. She tried to think the case through, but no conclusions would come.

Her father was sitting across the room reading the Sunday paper. He asked conversationally, "How's the investigation going?"

Nancy said, "I don't know. It's frustrating —it doesn't add up. Means. Motive. Opportunity. I can't get a clear picture of who's planning it all."

Carson folded the front section of the paper. "At least the robberies aren't on page one anymore. Brenda wrote another article about them, but it's buried on page twelve."

Nancy smiled. "Sounds like she hasn't come up with any new angles." Knowing Brenda, Nancy decided, she must have been feeling very frustrated. The reporter loved to see her byline on page one.

"No, she hasn't." Her father opened the business section. "On the other hand, the plunge in Hayward's stock price is top financial news."

Nancy went to see. Looking over his shoulder, she read that Hayward shares had now lost eighty percent of their value. Analysts were predicting that, barring a sudden change in fortune, the company would be bankrupt within a week.

"How awful," she groaned. "People are losing a ton of money just because of a couple of break-ins. And Tom's losing the most."

"Well, the ones who sell their shares are losing," Carson said.

Nancy suddenly stood upright. "Dad! What did you just say?"

"I said, the people who sell their shares at bargain prices are the losers. You see, a decline in a stock's price is really only a loss on paper. You have to sell to actually lose money."

"That's it!" Insight flooded Nancy's mind like a sudden burst of sunshine. She cried, "Dad, you just gave me the answer!"

"I did?"

Nancy threw her arms around his neck and kissed his cheek. "You said a drop in value is only a 'paper' loss, right?"

"Right."

129

"And isn't it also true that for every seller of stock there's a buyer?"

"True. A 'sale' is always an exchange between two parties," Carson agreed.

"Then that's it! Nancy exulted. "I've cracked the case!"

Chapter

Fourteen

THERE ARE just a few things I have to check," Nancy added. "Can you help me, Dad?"

"I'll try," Carson said. He was still in the dark, Nancy could see, but he trusted his daughter's abilities.

Nancy said, "I know the price of Hayward stock is down, but exactly how many people are selling their shares? A lot? A few? And how many people are doing the buying?"

"There's no way for us to know that for sure," her father explained. "But I can tell you how many shares have been sold this past week."

Carson turned the pages in the business section. "Here we are. The number of shares traded this week was—wow, two million!"

"That's a lot?"

"Nancy, there are only six million shares in existence, and Tom owns slightly more than half of those."

"So about two-thirds of the other shareholders have sold out," she calculated. "I wish there was *some* way to know for sure who was doing the buying."

Carson studied her. "You know, I think I see what you're getting at. If you can supply enough evidence, then the Securities and Exchange Commission can subpoena brokerage house records and prove who did the buying."

"Really? That's great!" Nancy said happily. "Maybe you can help me with something else, too."

"Shoot."

"How much of Loomis & Petersen does Stanley Loomis own?"

"That's easy," her father said. "Forty-nine percent. Just under half. Roy Petersen controls the firm."

"Dad, how do you know that?"

Carson smiled. "I'm their lawyer."

That left only one point for Nancy to check. She walked to the phone. She hated to make this call, but it was essential.

"Hello, Brenda?" she said, once the connection was made. "It's Nancy Drew."

"Hello, Nancy," Brenda said frostily. "How's the case going?"

"Uh, okay. But I need to ask you a question."

"Oh? Why should I help you out if you won't help me?" Brenda asked.

Nancy took a deep breath. This was the part she had dreaded. "Because I've got the case nailed down. I just need to fill in a few of the details."

"What do I get in return?" Brenda asked bluntly.

"Some exclusive details," Nancy offered, "once the arrest is made."

There was a pause. "Okay, you're on."

"How did you first hear about the break-in at the CD Revolution warehouse?" Nancy asked.

"An anonymous caller phoned the city desk and asked specifically for me," Brenda said with a touch of pride.

Nancy's heart leaped. "And then you gave that caller your home number, in case he wanted to give you any more tips, right?"

"How did you know that?" Brenda asked, surprised.

"It doesn't matter. Is that how you found out about the Jumping Jeans warehouse break-in the next day?"

"Yes. Now, when are the police going to make the arrest?" Brenda demanded.

"Soon," Nancy said evasively. "Thanks, Brenda. Bye."

She hung up quickly and immediately dialed again.

Chief McGinnis was against her plan. It was much too dangerous, he maintained.

Patiently Nancy explained that while she now knew the identity of the gang's mastermind, her evidence against him wouldn't hold up in court. To be sure of convicting him they needed a confession. And their man would not confess to the police. He was far too cool for that.

Their only hope, she argued, was to surprise a confession out of him. That meant that he had to be confronted by someone he didn't fear—someone who would catch him off guard.

By the time she finished, the chief had no choice but to agree.

Even though it was Sunday, the front doors of the Hayward Security building whooshed open to admit her. Nancy wasn't surprised. She had known that they would be working.

There was no receptionist, so she walked straight back to Neil Masterson's office. Inside, the special ribbonless computer printer was busily clacking away. Tom Hayward was sliding a cardboard box under Neil's desk.

"One of the laptop computers?" Nancy asked.

Tom straightened. Without pausing, he said, "Yes, it's a laptop. A present. A bonus, you might say."

Smart. Very smart, she thought. "Too bad Neil won't get to keep it," she said. "The police will take it as evidence against you."

"Oh?" Tom arched an eyebrow quizzically. "Evidence of what?"

So it was going to be like that. Nancy steeled herself. She had known that she would have to do this the hard way.

"I first became suspicious of you that night in the scrap metal yard when you miraculously 'saved' my life," she began.

"Yes, that was a lucky coincidence," Tom agreed.

"I'm not a big believer in coincidence, though," Nancy went on. "You knew exactly where to stand."

"Nancy, you seem to be accusing me of something here." He raised his shoulders and turned up his palms.

"You're right. I should start from the beginning," she said, trying to hide her nervousness. "It's a simple story, but it took me a long time to piece it together."

The printer stopped clacking.

"It begins with something my father said. About stocks," Nancy explained. "He said that if the price goes down you only lose money if you sell. That got me thinking."

"About what?" Tom asked. He sat down in Neil's desk chair.

Nancy's voice grew stronger. "About buying. It hit me that although selling means losing money, *buying* could mean earning money—lots of it—*if* the stock price went back up again. In fact, you could double, triple, or even quadruple your money."

"Naturally," Tom said. "But what of it?"

She had him now, she could tell. He was

stringing her along to find out how much she knew. Her confidence surged.

"You've been trying to buy out your main competitor, Loomis & Petersen, in order to get what you want."

"Which is?"

Nancy looked straight into his eyes. "A monopoly. The security business all to yourself."

Tom's eyes narrowed.

"Now, Petersen was willing to sell out," Nancy went on. "He's old. Probably getting ready to retire. But Loomis wouldn't sell. I found that out one day when I visited their offices."

Tom didn't move, but his gaze was hostile now.

"You needed money to buy Petersen's controlling interest," Nancy continued, "and you knew you could get it by buying Hayward stock low and selling it high. The only problem was how to push the price of the stock up and down."

A muscle in Tom's jaw twitched.

"That's where the robberies came in," Nancy explained. "They were bad publicity. Investors lost confidence. They sold. You bought, probably under another name. Once you had enough stock, your plan was to 'solve' the case, recover the stolen goods, and watch the stock price soar."

Finally Tom spoke. "You're saying *I* committed the robberies?"

"You and Adam Reeves," Nancy said. "At first I couldn't understand how a guy with a prison record could get hired at Hayward. Then I realized that you hired him yourself, before Neil Masterson started working here. He was willing to commit crimes for you when ordered," Nancy said. "You robbed your own customers with his help. But you didn't steal much. You didn't have to. Just enough to commit the crime."

Tom probed deeper. "And where are the goods now?"

"Probably stashed in another warehouse somewhere," Nancy guessed, "waiting to be 'discovered' by you at the right moment. That explains why none of us has been able to trace them."

Tom leaned back in his chair and pressed his fingertips together. "Okay, let's suppose your theory is correct. How did Adam and I arrange the break-ins? Adam only knew the code for the CD Revolution warehouse."

"Easy." Nancy glanced at the printer. "You just printed new envelopes and the computer assigned new codes. After the break-ins, you 'changed' the codes again for security reasons. No one knew they had been changed twice."

Tom nodded. "Clever. Seems you've figured out a flaw in the system."

"Stanley Loomis helped me with it," she admitted. "He told me that your system was as 'secure as a bureau drawer,' which anyone can open. I started from there."

"Go on."

Nancy took a deep breath. "There was only one more thing you needed—a fall guy. Someone to take the blame. You chose Neil. He has a motive. Plus he has the means. He could print new envelopes as easily as you. As for opportunity, he spends evenings with his family, but that's okay. The 'gang' took care of the robberies, Neil only cooperated with them. Which is enough to send him to prison, and which is why you are planting that laptop computer under his desk."

"Criminals," Tom said, "are so careless."

"Exactly. You even tried to point *me* at Neil, and for a while it worked. The evidence suggested he was guilty, but I couldn't square that with what I knew of his character. He's an honest man with a good reputation."

"But what about Stanley Loomis?" Tom said. *"He* has a sordid past."

"He reformed long ago," Nancy said. "His only problem now is competition from you. He was working on it, too, planning new products and services."

Tom waved his hand as if to dismiss her entire story. "That's all very interesting, Nancy, but you are forgetting one thing: I have alibis for the break-ins. So does Adam, for that matter. One time I was even with you!"

Nancy smiled. "Oh, yes—Career Day. That's where you got really clever. On Career Day you and Adam robbed the warehouse early in the morning. Then you tied Adam to the chair, where he stayed all day. You, meanwhile, established your alibi by speaking at the Career Fair with me and Chief McGinnis. Late in the afternoon, Adam tripped the emergency exit alarm and told his hair-raising story."

"But Adam had to phone in to our headquarters every hour. How did he do that?" Tom asked. His voice was rising in pitch.

"He didn't. A recording did. It's easy to rig up. You use the same equipment that's used to make junk phone calls. Every hour it dials the

Hayward number, plays a brief recording, and hangs up. It was the same trick you used the other night to make it seem like Adam was working when he was actually waiting for us. The equipment is probably at your house, right?"

Tom's jaw tightened. He was starting to sweat, Nancy saw with satisfaction. "Okay, Nancy, I'll admit this all sounds plausible. But so what? Neil Masterson or Stanley Loomis could have masterminded the robberies, too. There's as much evidence against either of them as there is against me."

"Not true," Nancy said calmly.

"What do you mean, it's not true!" He was shouting now. "Look at their motives! Neil's debts! Loomis's hatred of me!"

"Those are facts," Nancy agreed, "but you see, I am positive you are guilty because I know something about Neil and Loomis that you don't know. Neil is moonlighting for Loomis on the weekends. He's helping Loomis plan his new systems and services. I took secret pictures of one of their meetings yesterday."

"No!"

"It's true. And Loomis sends Neil checks that are made to the exact amount of Neil's hospital bills. I've seen them. All Neil and Loomis have to do to dismiss the case against them is tell the truth. By elimination, that will leave only one mastermind—you, Tom."

"No, no, *no!*" Tom pounded his fists on Neil's desktop. His face was red. "I knew I shouldn't have let you investigate."

He leaped up from his chair. Nancy was about to give a signal, when suddenly she was blinded by a bright light.

From the doorway an electronic flash bleached the scene white for a millisecond. Spots danced in front of Nancy's eyes.

"Nice going, Nancy," she heard Brenda say. "You got him cold. And I've got it all on tape! I was standing right outside. What a story this is going to make!"

"Yeah, some story," Tom said. As Nancy's vision cleared, she saw that he was holding a gun. "Too bad you won't ever get to write it, Brenda. Nancy, call off your backup!"

Chapter

Fifteen

How do you know I have a backup?" Nancy asked nervously. Having a gun pointed at her was not her favorite experience.

"Don't treat me like an idiot," Tom growled. "No way would you have pushed me so hard without a backup. Call 'em off!"

Nancy was wearing a blazer. Flipping up its lapel, she spoke into the tiny wireless microphone that was pinned there. "Chief, he's got a gun. We have to let him go."

"You mean, let *us* go," Tom clarified. Leaping across the desk, he ran behind Brenda, threw his elbow around her neck, and pressed the barrel of the gun to her temple. "Lois Lane, here, is going with me."

Brenda gasped, her face white with fear.

"Wait! Take me instead," Nancy offered.

"Oh, no! You're too smart," Tom said. "Brenda here was dumb enough to let me use her to spread bad publicity about my company, but I think she's smart enough to help me get away without causing any trouble."

"Yes, that's why you were so willing to talk to her at the Jumping Jeans warehouse," Nancy said, stalling for time. "I thought that was foolish then, but—"

"I'm no fool and neither are you," Tom said. "Now, keep back!"

He wrestled Brenda out of the office with his arm still around her throat and the gun still pressed to her temple. Nancy followed at a distance as he took Brenda outside to his BMW. He forced her in through the driver's side. Then he climbed in and slammed the door.

"So long, Nancy!" he called. The BMW roared to life.

Nancy looked around desperately. Down the road in either direction—out of sight from

inside the Hayward building but visible now
—were a dozen vans full of cops. They were
useless now. Tom had a hostage.

He took off. Making a sudden decision,
Nancy leaped into her Mustang and followed.
She didn't know where he was going, but no
way was she going to let him kidnap Brenda.

She caught up to him half a mile later. He
was heading in the direction of the airport. In
her rearview mirror Nancy saw the police vans
pulling up behind her. Good. She needed
backup for what she was about to do. They
couldn't let him get on an airplane with
Brenda!

Accelerating, she pulled up next to him and
jerked her wheel sideways.

Wham! Her car smacked into his.

Wham! She hit him again, and this time kept
swerving until he was forced first onto the
shoulder and then off the road, where he
skidded to a stop. Nancy stopped beside the
car and leaped out, yelling at the top of her
lungs. It was essential to distract Tom—to
keep his mind off Brenda!

It worked. Brenda leaped out of the passenger side and began to run. Tom snapped open
his door and climbed out. He looked first at
Brenda, then at Nancy, unable to decide whom

to deal with first. It was enough time. The police vans roared up.

In an instant several police officers were out and crouching in firing position. Tom dropped his automatic and raised his hands.

Nancy gave a whoop of joy and ran after Brenda to make sure that she was all right.

Two days later Nancy sat in Chief McGinnis's office with her father, Brenda, Brenda's father, Bess, George, and Cindy Larson.

"Morning, everyone," the chief said, striding in. "I have some news. Tom Hayward will be arraigned before a grand jury later this very morning."

Everyone applauded.

Carson spoke up. "I have some news, too. After Tom's arraignment, Neil Masterson will become the acting head of Hayward Security. I'm assembling a pool of backers—Loomis & Petersen among them—who will pump fresh capital into the company to help it out of its tailspin."

"That's great," Nancy said. "It would be a shame if after all his trouble Neil had to lose his job, too."

Mr. Carlton spoke up again. "I've got some

connections at the hospital, and they tell me that Neil's little girl, Tasha, should be okay. Her last operation was a success, so she won't need any more."

Nancy's eyes moistened. That was the best news yet.

"There's one thing I still don't understand," George said after a moment. "Nancy, how were Tom and Adam able to know where you were every minute of your surveillance?"

"They didn't. Not every minute. But they planted a small transmitter on my car—the type that tells you if your target is getting closer or farther away—and that helped."

"What about when you were on foot?" George asked.

"They tailed me a few times," Nancy explained.

"Adam's testimony is going to be devastating to Tom's defense," Carson observed.

The chief agreed. "Thank goodness he agreed to cooperate with us. That and the recorded confession we got from Nancy's hidden microphone will make the DA's job a lot easier."

"Nancy," Cindy asked, "how did you know about the transmitter planted on your car?"

"Come outside and I'll show you."

The group went outdoors, where the temperature was surprisingly more like summer than autumn. Nancy's car was in the parking lot. The dents that she had put in it ramming Tom's car were gone. It also had a new coat of paint. Blue, as always.

"Wow, that was fast!" Bess remarked.

"You bet. From now on, this car is getting nothing but TLC," Nancy promised.

"Oh, right," George drawled. "You'd better sell it to someone else."

"Anyway, about the transmitter," Nancy said. "They found it while they were doing the bodywork yesterday."

A few minutes later the group broke up. Carson returned to his law office, Brenda and her father to their paper, and Bess and George took off for the tennis courts. Nancy was left alone with Cindy when Chief McGinnis went for coffee.

"Can I give you a lift?" Nancy offered. "Where are you going?"

"History class," Cindy said. "It's a school day. I have to go back."

"Too bad," Nancy said sympathetically.

"Oh, no. I'm looking forward to school. After this case, it seems like paradise. One more time, Nancy, I'm sorry I put us in danger," she apologized. "And thanks."

"Forget it," Nancy said warmly. "Maybe you'll work with me again?"

"I don't know. I kind of doubt it," Cindy said, climbing into the Mustang's passenger seat. "It was interesting, but also—"

"Scary? Boring? Both?" Nancy climbed in and twisted the key.

"Both, and a lot more. What I mean, though, is that after this I think I'll just read about your cases in the paper, if that's okay. It was great to do it once, but I definitely think that detective work is for people who know what they're doing and love doing it!"

With a smile, Nancy released the brake and hit the gas. Her Mustang surged forward and blended into traffic.

She couldn't have agreed more.

Nancy's next case:

Nancy and George join Carson Drew on a visit to Anchorage shipping magnate Henry Wilcox, and they're thrilled by the idea of seeing Alaska. But the thrills quickly turn to chills when the police accuse Wilcox of using his ships to smuggle ivory—and George is kidnapped to warn Nancy off the case!

Although convinced of Henry Wilcox's innocence, Nancy uncovers a connection between the smuggling scheme and a dog sled race in which his son is a contestant. As race day nears, Nancy knows that she and George are the ones sledding on thin ice. She must find a way to unmask the smuggler before the trail to the ivory—and to her friend—goes cold . . . in *TRAIL OF LIES*, Case #53 in The Nancy Drew Files™.

Dear Friend,

Heard the latest? It seems just about everyone's talking about the sensational new series set in my hometown. It's called River Heights, and if you haven't heard, you don't know what you're missing!

You know I love to ask questions, so let me ask you a few. Do you like romance? A juicy secret? Do you believe there's life after homework? If so, take it from me, you'll love this exciting series starring the students of River Heights High.

I'd like you to meet Nikki Masters, all-American sweetheart of River Heights High, and Niles Butler, the gorgeous British hunk who makes Nikki's knees shake. And Brittany Tate, leader of the "in" crowd, who knows what she wants and will do just about anything to get it. She's got her eye on supersnob Chip Worthington. Samantha Daley, meanwhile, has fallen for Kyle Kirkwood. He's a social zero, but she's come up with a foolproof plan to turn him into the hottest ticket in town.

It's a thrill-filled world of teen dreams and teen schemes. It's all delicious fun, and it's all waiting for you—in River Heights!

Sincerely,
Nancy Drew

P.S. Turn the page for your own private preview of River Heights #9: *Lies and Whispers.*

Talk of the Town!

Brittany Tate, as devious as she is gorgeous, is out to snare the number-one country-club snob, Chip Worthington. He'd make the perfect boyfriend, her ticket to the top of the River Heights social scene. So what if she can hardly stand the guy?

Lacey Dupree can't forgive herself for the argument she had with boyfriend Rick Stratton just before his near-fatal rock climbing accident. Now that he's finally regained consciousness, the question that weighs most on her heart is, Will he ever forgive her?

Karen Jacobs has never loved any guy the way she loves Ben Newhouse. But the feeling can drive her to the depths of despair. Has Ben *really* gotten over his ex-girlfriend, model Emily Van Patten? And if not, how can Karen ever compete with someone so beautiful?

Ellen Ming is in trouble. Her father's been accused of embezzlement, and now Kim Bishop has accused Ellen of stealing junior class funds! Ellen's only hope is Nancy Drew. Will Nancy find a way to put a stop to the vicious gossip?

THE RUMORS ARE FLYING
IN RIVER HEIGHTS—
CATCH THEM IN
LIES AND WHISPERS!

"Hurry, Ben!" Lacey Dupree urged. "Can't you go any faster?"

"I'm doing the speed limit, Lacey," Ben Newhouse responded.

Lacey impatiently brushed back her halo of long red-gold waves and trained her eyes on the road ahead. Just one more block and they'd be at the hospital. One more block and she could see Rick Stratton, her boyfriend. Rick had finally regained consciousness after a rock-climbing accident.

Ben made a left turn into the hospital parking lot. Lacey opened her door as the car coasted to a stop.

"Whoa, Lacey!" Ben hit the brakes and turned to her. "I know you're anxious, but take it easy, okay?"

"I'm sorry, Ben," Lacey said as she opened the door wider. "I just can't wait. I have to see Rick!"

She slid out of the car and headed for the entrance. Across the lobby she skidded to a stop in front of the bank of elevators.

Jabbing the Up button impatiently, Lacey paused to

take a deep breath. Now that she was actually there, she started to worry again. What would Rick say when he saw her? He might hate her and blame her. If they hadn't had that terrible argument, he wouldn't have fallen during his rock-climbing expedition. He wouldn't have been lying unconscious in the hospital for more than two weeks!

The elevator doors slid open, and Lacey sprang on. She tapped her foot the whole time the elevator rose. As soon as the doors parted, she stepped out.

She thought of how she'd come there, day after day, her heart breaking at the sight of Rick lying unconscious. The pain of it had been hard to bear. But how would it compare to the pain of Rick's rejecting her now?

Rick's door was open. Lacey peeked in. Rick was pale, and there were dark circles under his eyes. His muscular body seemed thin now. He looked ill, Lacey thought, but he'd never looked so good to her.

He glanced up just then. "Lacey," he said.

"Hello, Rick." Lacey couldn't seem to move from the doorway. Did he want her to go to him? She didn't know what to do!

"Oh, Rick," Lacey whispered, her eyes blurring with tears. "I'm so glad you're back."

Couples! Everywhere Brittany Tate looked, she saw nothing but couples. When she got off the school bus, she almost crashed into Mark Giordano and Chris Martinez, king and queen of the jocks. Nikki Masters, the golden girl, was just pulling into a parking space with that adorable Niles Butler. From across the quad, Robin Fisher waved to Nikki and Niles with her boyfriend, Calvin Roth.

Brittany pressed her lips together as she headed up the walk. Robin had really spoiled things for her at the Winter Carnival Ball. She'd let Brittany have it for setting up a fight between Lacey Dupree and Rick Stratton. Robin had actually blamed Brittany for Rick's accident! It was bad enough that Brittany herself had felt guilty for her part in the couple's fight. She didn't need Robin to rub it in. And she certainly didn't need Tim Cooper to hear about it!

He'd been standing in the shadows, listening to every word. The rest of the night had been a disaster. Tim had been icily polite, but it was obvious he wished he was a million miles away. And he'd dumped Brittany on her doorstep like a load of old laundry.

She had come so close to having Tim for a boyfriend. She'd turned over a new leaf and been incredibly nice, and Tim had finally responded. But now Tim thought she was a double-dealing snake.

Brittany would never forgive Robin Fisher. Never. She gave Robin her trademark drop-dead look as she walked by. Robin merely grinned back at her. Brittany tossed her gleaming dark hair and hurried over to Kim Bishop and Samantha Daley, her best friends.

"What's going on with you and Robin?" Kim asked. "I saw that look you gave her."

Brittany shrugged. "That girl should get a life. She didn't like the fact that I went to the ball with her best friend's ex-boyfriend."

Samantha Daley leaned closer, her cinnamon eyes sparkling. "What *did* happen with you and Tim?" she asked in her soft southern drawl.

Kim and Samantha were staring expectantly. Brittany thought fast. She leaned over and said in a whisper, "I'll tell you a secret. That hunk Tim Cooper is just the teeniest bit boring. Nikki can have him." Brittany shook back her thick, dark hair and laughed. "I'm looking for someone a little wilder."

Normally, that comment would impress Samantha and Kim. They'd demand more details, wondering what she was planning. But Samantha and Kim were barely listening to her. They were staring over her head.

"Here come the guys," Kim said.

Brittany turned around. Jeremy Pratt and Kyle Kirkwood, Kim and Samantha's boyfriends, were heading for them. Kyle's face brightened at the sight of Samantha. Brittany wanted to throw up.

"Hello, gorgeous," Jeremy said to Kim. She smiled regally. The two of them were such a pain, Brittany thought impatiently. They thought they were the hottest thing to hit River Heights High since Mexican Day in the cafeteria.

"We were just talking about the country club dance this weekend," Jeremy said. "It's going to be major."

"It sounds okay," Kyle said. "I'm not a big fan of the country club, but Samantha really wants to go."

"I can't wait," Samantha said. She slipped her hand into Kyle's.

Brittany tuned them out. She was glad to be reminded of the country club dance. It would be the first big function she would attend as a member. It was time, Brittany decided, for her to be back on top. That meant snaring a fantastic new boyfriend.

"Who's going?" she asked Jeremy.

"Oh, the usual country club crowd," Jeremy said, waving a hand. "No one you'd know."

Brittany's hand tightened on her books. Jeremy

was so slimy he must have crawled out of a swamp. He never let her forget that she had only recently become a member—and only a junior member at that.

"Some of the college crowd will probably be there," Kim added.

Brittany sighed. "I'm sick of the college crowd," she said. "Jack Reilly called the other night, but I refused to speak to him. Who else is going, Kim?"

"The snobs from Talbot and Fox Hill, of course," Kim replied. Talbot and Fox Hill were the boys' and girls' private schools in River Heights.

"I just hope Chip Worthington isn't there," Jeremy muttered.

Brittany stifled a grin. Kim had told her that Chip had nearly rearranged the aristocratic Pratt profile a while ago. She could understand why Jeremy wouldn't want to see him again.

"You could always hire a bodyguard, Jeremy," Brittany said sweetly.

"It's not that I'm afraid of him," Jeremy returned quickly. "He makes all these comments about Kim, just to give me grief. He keeps leering at her and saying things like, 'What are you doing with the most beautiful girl in River Heights, Pratt?' Stuff like that. It's totally annoying."

"Really," Kim agreed, tossing her shiny blond hair.

Jeremy might hate it, but Kim wasn't too upset, Brittany was sure. Who wouldn't like being called the most beautiful girl in River Heights? Of course, Chip Worthington hadn't met Brittany Tate yet.

Then it hit her. Why not go after Chip? Brittany was bored with all the boys at school. Why not stake out some new territory? Let Kim and Jeremy be king and queen of River Heights High. Brittany and Chip would run the town!

Ellen Ming walked to the student council meeting. She took her usual seat and waited for Ms. Rose, the student council faculty advisor, to show up.

While she waited, Ellen began to feel uneasy. She saw Juliann Wade, the treasurer of the student council, whisper something to Patty Casey, who was the secretary. They both glanced at Ellen, then quickly looked away.

Ben Newhouse arrived, and then Kevin Hoffman came in. Kevin grinned warmly at Ellen as he slid into his seat.

Feeling a blush start on her cheeks, Ellen stared down at the tabletop. Sometimes the feelings she'd had when she had her crush on Kevin came back. Nothing had ever come of her silly crush, not even one date. Ellen knew she was too serious for Kevin, who was full of jokes and mischief. There was something about his unruly red-brown hair and easy grin that made her smile.

Ms. Rose walked into the room with her brisk step. "Good afternoon, people. Let's get started," she said. "Today the first item on the agenda is the proposal for a luau. A committee has already been formed, headed by Ellen Ming. Since the committee will be mainly using the decorations from the tropical theme that we scrapped for the Winter Carnival, the cost won't be too high. And the committee has high hopes that the record and tape sales will take care of the rest of the costs. Ellen, how's the whole plan going?"

"Fine," Ellen said. "We have volunteers lined up to handle the record and tape sales."

"Sounds great. Keep us posted," Ms. Rose said. She studied her notes again. "Now, if there's nothing else on the luau, let's get to—"

"Ms. Rose?" Juliann Wade waved her hand in the air.

Ms. Rose looked up. "Yes, Juliann?"

"I was wondering who's handling the proceeds from the record sale."

Ms. Rose frowned at Juliann, but she turned to Ellen. "Ellen?"

Ellen saw Patty Casey poke Juliann underneath the table. Ellen's heart began to flutter. "I am," she said in a shaky voice.

"What's your point, Juliann?" Ms. Rose asked frostily. Ellen had a feeling Ms. Rose knew what the girl was getting at—and she didn't like it.

Juliann shook back her blond hair defiantly. "I'm just wondering if we should reconsider having Ellen handle the funds, that's all. I'd be glad to take over."

"I agree with Juliann," Patty said quickly.

Ms. Rose studied the two girls. "And what exactly do you agree with, Patty?"

Patty's eyes traveled around the room as if she was seeking an answer. "Well, that maybe Juliann should take charge of the funds. She *is* school treasurer."

Juliann nodded. "Especially under the circumstances . . ." she said meaningfully, letting her voice trail off.

The room was quiet. Did that mean that people were shocked or that they agreed with Juliann? Ellen felt sick. How could this be happening? They thought she wasn't trustworthy enough to take charge of the money!

She felt Ben stir next to her, but before he could say anything, Kevin Hoffman spoke up.

"That's very nice of you, Juliann." Kevin's voice was calm, but it held a deadly undertone Ellen had never heard before. "Ellen *has* been doing two jobs since Lacey Dupree has dropped out temporarily. She could feel overloaded. I'm sure those were the circumstances you were talking about, right?"

Juliann swallowed. She glanced at Ms. Rose, who was giving her a cold stare. "Of course," she mumbled.

"But Ellen is doing such a fantastic job," Kevin went on steadily, "as usual, that as long as she feels she can handle it, I see no reason to make a change. Do you feel you can handle this on top of Lacey's responsibilities, Ellen?"

Ellen looked at Kevin. His green eyes had a fierce look. He nodded at her, giving her courage. He was on her side! "Yes," she managed to choke out.

"Then let's not waste any more time," Ms. Rose stated crisply. "We have more important business."

Everyone in the room relaxed, except for Ellen. Her heart was racing. Kevin had saved her neck, all right, but she couldn't get over the fact that Juliann had been so cruel in the first place.

Suddenly Ellen realized that she hadn't thought of the worst thing about her father's being accused of embezzlement. He might not go to jail, but his life still could be destroyed. He would always be under a cloud of suspicion.

Ellen had just seen something she wished she hadn't. People could take a rumor or a suspicion and they could use it to disgrace someone. If Ellen was facing that kind of attitude in a student council meeting, what would Mr. Ming face at work? Ellen shivered with foreboding. Things could get a lot worse before they got better.

Brittany scanned the crowd at the country club dance.

"Who are you looking for?" Samantha asked.

"I'm just shopping, Samantha dear," Brittany said distractedly. But just as she finished speaking, she caught sight of Chip Worthington. He was tall and seemed assured, as if he owned the country club. He scanned the room with a bored air.

Brittany willed him to turn around and look at her, but he turned his attention to his friends. She sighed. She'd have to get Kim to introduce her.

Brittany saw her chance. Kim and Jeremy were standing on the sidelines, having a soda. Brittany watched as Chip joined them. Jeremy's face darkened in a scowl, but Chip was grinning as he talked. He was probably tormenting Jeremy, Brittany thought. Maybe Chip wasn't so bad, after all.

Quickly Brittany walked across the room to Kim and Jeremy.

"Hi," she interrupted breathlessly. "I haven't had a chance to talk to you guys all night." She fixed her dark eyes on Chip. "Oh, I'm sorry, am I interrupting?"

"Not at all," Chip said. His clear green eyes flicked over her, and he gave a lazy grin. "Not at all," he repeated. "Who are *you,* and why haven't I met you yet?"

Brittany smiled back. "How about meeting me right now?" she said. "I'm Brittany Tate."

"Chip Worthington," Chip answered.

Kim stirred beside Brittany. She might not be able to stand Chip, but it was clear she didn't like Brittany stealing his attention, either. "Brittany became a junior member of the club recently," she said. "That's probably why you don't know her."

"I suppose you go to school with Pratt, here," Chip said. He casually ran a hand through his straight, side-parted brown hair.

"That's right. Do you go to Talbot?"

"Of course," Chip replied. "If every Worthington didn't enroll, the school would collapse and sink right into the ground. We practically built the place back in the Stone Age. Now we just throw pots of money at it to keep it running."

Brittany laughed her silvery laugh. What a snob! she thought. Kim was right, for once. "Well, thank heavens you enrolled, then," she said. "We wouldn't want anything to happen to Talbot."

"For sure," Chip agreed lazily. "And what do you do at River Heights High, Brittany?"

"Well, I'm on the school paper, the *Record,*" Brittany said. "I have my own column, called 'Off the Record.'"

"Nice name," Chip said.

Why did every remark he made sound as though he was making fun of her? Brittany wondered. But his eyes were definitely expressing approval. Did he like her or not?

Nikki Masters parked her car and followed Ellen Ming into the coffee shop. After they ordered sodas, Nikki looked at her expectantly.

"What's on your mind, Ellen?" Nikki leaned forward, her hands cupping her glass. Her blue eyes were kind and patient.

Ellen suddenly felt afraid. Nikki Masters had been in trouble once—that was true. But she was well past it now. She was beautiful and popular, and nice, too. Would she be able to sympathize with Ellen's problem?

"Ellen, if it makes it any easier for you, I know what it's like to need help," Nikki said softly. "I know it's hard to ask. But believe me, it's better. I want to do what I can."

Ellen's fears dissolved under the balm of Nikki's soft words. She gripped her glass and poured out her story, barely pausing for breath.

"I've gone over the junior class bank account more times than you can imagine," Ellen concluded. "I discovered right away that two deposits I recorded in the ledger didn't match the bank's record of deposits."

"How do you make the deposits?" Nikki asked. "At the bank?"

"No, it closes at three, so I use the night deposit slot," Ellen told her. "The two deposits were from last Friday and this Monday—from the record and tape sale. Each day I totalled the receipts, filled out a deposit slip, and sealed the envelope. Then I locked it in a drawer in the student council office. After school, I took it to the bank."

Nikki nodded thoughtfully. "So somebody got to the money while it was in the drawer. The person took out the bills and resealed the envelope.

"That's what I figure," Ellen said. "But, Nikki, who's going to believe that it wasn't me? After what's happened with my father, I mean."

"I believe it wasn't you," Nikki assured her. "Others will, too. Not everybody is like Kim Bishop, Ellen."

"But I'm class treasurer, Nikki. If my name isn't cleared, I'll lose the office."

"I have an idea," Nikki said slowly. "Would you mind if one more person knew the story? Not someone from school," she added hastily.

"Who?" Ellen asked, puzzled.

"Nancy Drew. She's a good friend of mine, and she lives next door."

"Wow," Ellen breathed. "Do you think it would be okay?"

"We won't know until I call her," Nikki said briskly. She reached into the pocket of her jeans for some change. "Can I?"

"Right now?" Ellen gulped. "I guess so. After all, how can I turn down a world-famous detective?"

Want more? Get the whole story in
River Heights #9, *Lies and Whispers.*